A Thankful Heart

A Thankful Heart

A Love at the Chocolate Shop Romance

Melissa McClone

TULE
PUBLISHING

Dedication

To CJ Carmichael for creating Sage and Copper Mountain Chocolates and my fellow Love at the Chocolate Shop authors who love books and chocolate as much as I do: Debra Salonen, Roxanne Snopek, Steena Holmes, and Marin Thomas!

Special thanks goes to: Laura Hyde Wines, animal rescuer extraordinaire with *A.R.K. Animals Require Kare*; to the *West Columbia Gorge Humane Society* for bringing beloved family members and special foster cats into our lives; to Jan Herinckx and *PSNEA* who do so much for Norwegian Elkhound rescue dogs, and finally; to Kimberly Field, Tina Jones, and Terri Reed for their support and friendship. Any mistakes about animal rescue operation or procedures are mine!

Chocolate is better than men, and so are dogs. At least, that's what Dakota Parker tells herself as she mends her broken heart and finds forever homes for rescue animals. So far, so good. She can indulge her love of chocolate where she works while her foster dogs provide her with the unconditional love she craves. What more does she need?

Seattle architect Bryce Grayson is counting the days until he can return home to the big city with his father in tow. That is if he can convince his dad to leave Montana. Bryce's escape plan, however, goes astray when he meets Dakota. Her sweet kisses put the chocolate she sells to shame. Maybe he should be the one to move to Marietta, but could he be happy living in such a small town?

He has until Thanksgiving to decide.

Chapter One

A CHOCOLATE LOVER'S ambrosia. That was what Dakota Parker called the hot chocolate on the Copper Mountain Chocolates' menu. She loved preparing the beverage for customers as well as herself. Decadent and delicious and dangerous to diets, but worth every calorie. It was also much better for her than falling for the wrong man again.

Hot chocolate—okay, any chocolate—and the rescue animals she helped find forever homes for were all she needed to be happy.

At least for now.

Standing behind the retail counter, Dakota stirred the chocolate, cream, and cinnamon mixture simmering on the stovetop against the wall. The mouthwatering scent tantalized her nose and taste buds. The shop's owner, Sage Carrigan O'Dell, kept the amount of each ingredient secret, but that didn't stop others, including Dakota, from trying to replicate the drink recipe at home.

And failing.

Big time.

That only kept people coming back.

Today's chilly autumn weather was bringing in more customers, so many that Dakota and her co-worker Portia Bishop, who had come in early to rotate stock now that November had arrived, could barely keep up with the hot chocolate orders. Sage was in the back making chocolate as she did each day, but she'd had to help out at the counter a few times.

Unexpected for a Tuesday.

Dakota had skipped her morning break and taken only fifteen minutes for lunch because the shop was so busy. It was just enough time to run home to take care of the dogs.

The bell on the door jingled.

She glanced over her shoulder to see three women from Bozeman leaving the shop. Each held a shopping bag. The women visited Marietta monthly to buy chocolate and have lunch. "Have a wonderful afternoon and a safe drive home."

Elise, a forty-year-old mother of a teenager and a toddler, looked over. "We'll see you in December."

Dakota grinned. "We'll be ready for you."

That brought laughter.

As Elise followed her friends outside, a man and a woman entered. A gust of cold air followed them inside.

Dakota shivered and set the wooden spoon on the copper-plated rest. "Welcome to Copper Mountain Chocolates."

The man grinned. "You mean this shop isn't called chocolate heaven?"

"Heaven, nirvana, Shangri-la. Take your pick," Dakota said.

His hair was more salt than pepper, and his face was tan, as if he spent the majority of his time outdoors. Given his worn green field jacket, he likely did. He glanced around before letting out a low whistle. "So many choices."

The woman nodded. She looked to be around the same age as the man, maybe a year or two younger. Her red wool coat complimented her clear complexion and bobbed blond hair. "A good thing we're in town for the rest of the week, so we can come back."

The man pointed at something in the window display and then walked up to the counter.

Dakota raised a tray containing chocolates handcrafted by Sage and offered a piece using a silver tong. "We're sampling champagne truffles today. Please feel free to try one."

Each took a truffle.

The woman took a bite. "Amazing."

Portia hurried out of the kitchen, aka the chocolate factory, to clear two of the four small tables where customers could enjoy their hot cocoa and chocolates. Her long ponytail bounced. The sleeves of her shirt were pushed up to her elbows.

The man scanned the menu. "We'd like two hot chocolates, please."

"Excellent choice," Dakota said in her happy-to-serve-you voice. Not that doing so took any effort. She loved everything about her job from the swoon-worthy chocolates to the store's cocoa and vanilla themed décor. She rang up the order, and the man paid.

He studied the photographs hanging on the wall. Each illustrated a step in how cocoa beans were processed and turned into the chocolate the shop sold.

The woman peered at the glass display case. "Does the store always smell this good?"

"Yes." Dakota grabbed two mugs. Uh-oh. They were running low. "It's a good thing the aroma has no calories or I'd never fit into my jeans."

The woman smiled. "Must be tempting being surrounded by so much chocolate."

"Very."

One of Dakota's favorite parts of working here was interacting with customers. "My coworker Rosie allows herself only one thing a day, but I don't have that kind of willpower. I love chocolate too much. That's why I take my foster dogs on daily walks no matter what the weather. I need the exercise as much as they do."

The woman's smile spread. "That's great you foster. We adopted a dog and a cat from a local shelter in Denver. Best decision ever. They make our house a home."

"I'm sure they do." Dakota wanted all rescue animals to find loving families. Having that dream didn't mean she was unrealistically optimistic.

I read your Home for the Holidays proposal. It's simplistic—more of a wish list than a plan to be implemented. This isn't a fantasyland with pet unicorns and never-ending rainbows. You're being unrealistically optimistic. You'll never find homes for all the rescue's animals by Christmas. If you want me to present your plan to the board of directors to get funding for a specific adoption effort, rewrite your proposal with a reasonable time frame, workable action plan with measurable milestones, and achievable goals.

Lori Donovan, the rescue director, rarely minced words and hadn't during their meeting yesterday, but what she'd said kept Dakota awake last night. The words still stung today.

Especially having the plan called simplistic.

The word made Dakota feel inadequate. She might not be brilliant like her older brother York, who was a computer genius in the Air Force, or her younger sister Nevada, who was getting a PhD at Columbia, but Dakota wasn't stupid. She just had to work harder than they did.

And most everyone else.

But this wasn't the time or place to throw herself a pity party. Dakota focused on her customers. "Would you like anything else?"

The man's gaze went from the photographs to her. "Could we have extra whipped cream on our drinks and lots of chocolate on top?"

"Of course." She motioned to the four small tables surrounded by chairs on the other side of the shop. All were clean thanks to Portia. "If you'd like to take a seat, I'll bring over the hot chocolates when they're ready."

"Thank you," the woman said, and the couple headed to a table.

Portia, twenty-two with a pretty face and a flair for style, carried a plastic bin with mugs and dessert-sized plates that had held chocolates. Sage was not only their boss and resident chocolatier, but she was also Portia's aunt.

"Not sure how long the tables will stay clean with so many customers coming in."

She wore the same indigo blue shirt and dark jeans as Dakota. Portia had recommended the clothing to offset the copper-colored aprons that left Dakota feeling washed out with her light brown hair and fair skin tone. Their coworker Rosie was much happier with the new work uniform, too.

"I'm so glad you're feeling better this week. I don't know what I would have done if you hadn't come in early today." Using a ladle, Dakota filled the first mug with the thick, creamy mixture. "Even with Sage here, too, I haven't had time to do anything but ring up sales and serve hot chocolate."

"I'm happy to be here. I want to work as many hours as I can. I'll wash another load of mugs so we don't run out."

"Good idea. We only have three left." Dakota filled the second mug. "With the temperature dropping, things might not slow down for a while."

That was okay. She enjoyed chatting with regular customers and meeting new ones. Offering a free chocolate sample not only brightened someone's day, but it also worked as an ideal icebreaker, especially with the quieter folks.

By focusing on others, she could push aside her own troubles. Perfect for a day like today when she didn't want to think about having to rewrite the rescue proposal. The thought of doing so intimidated her. The first version had taken weeks to put together.

"I'll take care of the mugs and be right back." Portia adjusted her hands on the bin. "Yell if you need help."

Dakota added a spiral tower of whipped cream on each mug, and then she sprinkled a double batch of chocolate shavings over the top.

She carried the cups to the couple who sat with their gazes locked on each other. Their entwined hands rested on top of the table.

A lump formed in her throat.

So sweet.

Maybe Dakota would find a man to hold hands and make goo-goo eyes with over hot chocolate. Someone nice and respectful, who thought dogs and cats were wonderful, not nuisances, had to be out there. She just didn't know where.

Face it. She'd been falling for all the wrong guys—workaholics, players, cheaters, and self-centered ones.

No more.

Her heart had healed after her fiancé, Craig Wilkins, broke up with her minutes before their wedding ceremony was supposed to begin. He'd blamed her long hours with the animal rescue and not wanting to spend the rest of his life covered in dog and cat hair. But that had only been his excuse at the time. She later discovered he'd met someone else.

Having to announce to the guests in the pews that a wedding wouldn't be taking place because Craig had bolted from the church, and then having to return gifts because she didn't trust him to do it with a polite note attached, would make anyone wary of relationships—both casual and serious ones. Was it any wonder she preferred the company of animals to men? Until she had faith in her ability to choose a decent guy—he didn't have to be perfect—she wanted to hold off on dating.

"Here you go." Dakota set the mugs on the table. Not a drop spilled, but after working at the shop for three years, she was an expert hot chocolate server. She removed napkins from her apron pocket and placed them on the table. "Enjoy."

"We will," the man said. "I have a feeling this place will be our hangout while we're in town."

"I hope so." She worked at the shop on Tuesdays, Wednesdays, and Thursdays. The other days, she spent volunteering at the rescue shelter. "Tomorrow, we'll be sampling the to-die-for 72% *Criollo* single-origin bar."

The woman raised her hot chocolate. The large diamond ring and matching wedding band on her left hand sparkled beneath the overhead lighting.

Dakota's left hand, especially her ring finger, felt barer than usual. A woman from nearby Livingston now wore the engagement ring Craig had asked Dakota to give back to him. According to her best friend Kelly Hamilton, Dakota had been too nice in returning the ring. She should have taken it to a pawnshop and donated the money to the animal rescue instead.

"Tomorrow is our thirty-fifth wedding anniversary." The woman sighed. "Having to-die-for chocolate sounds like the perfect way to celebrate."

"Congratulations," Dakota said.

The man lifted his wife's hand and brushed his lips across her knuckles. "Can't wait for the next thirty-five."

The woman gazed into her husband's eyes. "Me, either."

Awww. The two reminded Dakota of her parents. They had celebrated thirty-three years of marriage in March. Her mom claimed love conquered all. Dakota wasn't convinced, but she hoped her mom was right.

Time would tell.

Neither of her two siblings had married, so at least she hadn't disappointed her mom over not being in a committed relationship. If only Dakota could say that about the rest of her life here in Marietta. She loved her family, but none had understood the decisions she'd made. Her mother still wanted her to apply to law school.

Back behind the counter, she gave the pot of hot chocolate another stir. No one was outside the front window or by the door. She picked up a pen.

She would use the free time to finally mark down prices on the molded Halloween-themed chocolates. The chocolate was as delicious to eat as it was yesterday, but the pumpkin, bat, and ghost shapes were no longer in season now that November had arrived.

The bell above the door rang.

So much for free time. She set the pen on the counter.

A man walked in. Another burst of cold air came into the shop and brought goose bumps, but he quickly closed the door.

"Welcome to Copper Mountain Chocolates," she greeted as she always did.

His shoulders were angled toward the opposite side of the shop, so she couldn't see his face. Not everyone came right to the counter. Sometimes, people entered out of curiosity or to window shop. Others wanted a free sample or to warm up from the cold.

Dakota stirred the pot but found herself watching him.

He brushed a gloved hand through his sandy-blond hair. The short, messy style appealed to her more than the way he dressed.

An expensive-looking leather jacket showed off wide shoulders. A white collar peeked out the top. His khakis were creased. That amused her since she didn't own an iron. A pair of polished loafers completed his outfit.

His attire screamed big city.

Definitely not from around here.

No tie, but he reminded her more of the men she'd dated who worked inside, often behind desks in offices, and wore ties. She preferred men who worked outdoors.

Cowboys.

A man who faced the elements every day, had a strong work ethic, appreciated animals, and knew how to treat a woman appealed to her at a gut level. The boots and jeans they wore were an added bonus. Not that she'd dated a cowboy or wanted to date one now.

She focused on the man, letting her curiosity and imagination run wild.

Maybe he was a tourist from the east eager for a taste of the west.

Maybe he was a CEO taking a break from a high-pressure job by escaping to a small town that moved at a snail's pace.

Maybe he was a witness in a big case for the FBI and hiding out until it was time to testify at the trial.

Or maybe, and most likely, he was here because he liked chocolate.

"Would you like to try a champagne truffle?" She readied the tongs. "That's what we're sampling today."

He turned.

Her gaze collided with a pair of killer baby blues that made her breath catch and birds sing. Well, birds would be singing if there were any in the shop. A good thing she hadn't lifted the tray or the truffles would be all over the counter.

He was, in a word, stunning.

Dakota hoped she wasn't staring openmouthed or drooling, but she found him as appealing as her favorite Sage creation—dark chocolate with almond and cherry bits.

His slightly crooked nose gave him character, making his handsome face more interesting and rugged. A nice contrast to his smooth skin. Dakota was a fan of the razor-stubble look, but perhaps there was something to be said for clean-shaven.

He stared at Dakota. "What?"

She held the tray and used the silver tongs to offer him a piece. Thankfully, her hands were steady. "Would you like to try a sample?"

Or me.

Whoops. Where had that come from?

"No, thank you," he said.

She must be more tired than she realized, but that was what happened after a sleepless night worrying about her proposal and the animals. "The chocolate is processed here by our shop's owner. The best in Montana."

"No, thanks."

His full lips—how had she missed those?—parted. So

sexy.

Dakota stared, mesmerized. She would love to see how he ate a piece of chocolate. Would he nibble on one edge, take a bite, or chomp the piece in half?

"Are you sure you wouldn't want a taste?" she asked.

"I don't like chocolate."

Huh? Dakota knew better than to be annoyed by a customer, but that was exactly how she felt. *Don't react.* She kept a practiced smile on her face. "Copper Mountain Chocolates are special. Everybody likes them."

He shrugged. "Guess I'm not everybody. Sell anything else?"

Who was this guy? And why was he here if he didn't like chocolate? "Hot chocolate."

"That's not so bad, but I don't have time. I have a list of what I'd like to buy." He thumbed the screen on his phone. "Two fudge truffles, two milk chocolate salted caramels, and a piece of the dark chocolate cherry hazelnut bark."

He might not be from around here or like chocolate, but his order contained top-selling items. Strange.

Dakota placed the candy in a bag and rang up his order. She told him the amount.

He pulled out a leather billfold that was as fancy and polished as his shoes.

Anticipation built. He could be anyone passing through town, but she would soon know his name from his credit card.

He scanned the shop with a cursory glance, pulled out a twenty, and handed it to her.

So much for finding out who he was.

Strangely disappointed, she gave him the change and his bag of chocolates. "Enjoy the rest of your day."

"You, too." He opened the door and looked back at her. "Nice shop."

With that, he walked out onto Main Street and passed in front of the big window.

She watched him.

Did the guy have a better-than-you attitude or was he merely distracted? Maybe a combination of both?

Either way, Dakota found him interesting. A little...intriguing.

Warning bells sounded.

No. No. No.

Dakota would not allow herself to be intrigued by any man, let alone a stranger. She had no idea who the guy was. For all she knew, he could be the worst possible Mr. Wrong, a combination of those who'd come before *and* allergic to pet dander. He could be a psycho stalker. Or worse.

Time to phone Kelly and meet for a session of their Chocolate Is Better Than Men Club, aka CIBTMC. Chocolate and a girls' night at Grey's Saloon was a wonderful combination. A good time, too, even if she and Kelly were the only club members due to everyone else falling in love. Still, a CIBTMC meeting would get Dakota's mind where it should be—off men.

Including handsome, nameless strangers buying chocolate they didn't eat.

Chapter Two

STARING OUT HIS father's living room window at the gray sky overhead, Bryce Grayson knew one thing—November would be the longest month of his life.

No cars on the street. No people on the sidewalk. No signs of life outside his father's house.

The muscles in Bryce's neck bunched into marble-like balls. He fought the urge to groan. This would be rush hour back home in Seattle, but not here in the middle of nowhere Marietta. If boredom didn't kill him, the quiet would.

Still, spending the month with his dad was the right decision, even if Chelsea Fordham, the software project manager he'd been dating, had been less than understanding. She didn't want to be put second, even though his father needed help.

When she'd issued an ultimatum to keep Bryce from heading to Montana, he'd told her to find someone who could put her first. Funny thing was he didn't miss her and had only occasionally thought of her since then. A good thing he *hadn't* taken that relationship further.

His friends, who'd gone from one half of a happy couple to divorce court, made Bryce think marriage wasn't for everyone, including him. He'd spent too many nights listening to the woes of the recently split or newly divorced, which had only soured him on making the ultimate commitment with a woman. He'd thought Chelsea wasn't interested in anything serious based on what she'd said.

Lip service.

Now he had one less distraction in his life. He could focus on his dad and the proposal he would submit when he returned to Seattle. It could be a huge opportunity for his design firm.

A pickup truck drove past. That was the first vehicle he'd seen since walking home from Main Street earlier. "Not a lot of people out."

"That's why I love this town," his dad said in a contented tone. "So peaceful."

Bryce faced his father, who sat in a worn leather recliner with a brand-new wheelchair on the right. Casts covered both of his legs. He'd sustained the broken bones from a fall off a ladder at one of his construction sites. According to Dr. Jack Gallagher, Walt Grayson was lucky to be alive.

Lucky.

The word gave Bryce nightmares.

His dad had always seemed larger than life, invincible even after the death of his mom four years ago. But now…

Bryce rubbed his eyes, blinked, and then refocused.

"Doesn't seem like there's much to do around here."

"There's enough," his dad said.

It didn't seem that way to Bryce, but that wasn't the reason he wanted his father to recognize the downfalls of the small town he now called home. Montana was closer than Pennsylvania, where Bryce had grown up, but living so far apart from each other wasn't working. He needed his father to be closer, both in times of emergency and day to day. "Maybe if you're into cow tipping."

"Marietta isn't like Seattle."

"Totally different."

Bryce missed the noise, the rain, the bumper-to-bumper traffic. Marietta couldn't compare to the vibrant, cosmopolitan city he'd called home during his four years of college and the ten years since then. He walked to the recliner, picked up the fleece blanket that had fallen onto the hardwood floor, and covered his father so he wouldn't catch a chill.

Somehow, Bryce would find a way to survive the month and convince his father to leave Marietta after Thanksgiving. "More cows and horses than people."

"Most of the time, yes, but during the rodeo and the Christmas stroll, the streets are jam-packed with people."

From one extreme to another.

No, thank you.

A town this size couldn't handle the influx of crowds, cars, or additional livestock. "Hard to imagine."

"If you stay longer, you won't have to imagine it."

The challenge in his dad's words brought a smile to Bryce's face. He expected no less from his father. "I have a better idea. Come to Seattle and see how much the city has to offer. Not just for Christmas but year round."

"I'm happy where I am." His dad didn't hesitate with his answer.

Not unexpected, but heat rose inside Bryce. His fingers curled. "With two broken legs?"

"Could have happened to anyone."

"It happened to you." Remembering the call from the Marietta hospital made Bryce's stomach churn. He'd never forget the panic. Waiting at the airport for a flight to Bozeman had made him feel useless. Reaching his father quickly wasn't possible. "Might be time to make some changes."

The lines on his father's face deepened. "Changes?"

"Cut back on your workload. Consider retiring."

The corners of his dad's mouth curved downward. "You make sixty-two sound ancient. I'm as capable and fit as I was at forty."

"I'm not saying you're old."

Bryce couldn't push too hard. Walt Grayson was mule stubborn when he wanted to be. This house was a perfect example. His father had made a fortune when he sold their luxurious family home and his successful construction firm, yet he'd chosen to purchase a modest three-bedroom, one-story house instead of a Victorian mansion over on Bramble Lane or one of the luxurious log houses outside of town.

Still, Bryce wanted to start the conversation while he had the chance. "But climbing ladders and working on rooftops might be better left to the younger people on your crew."

"I'd leave it to you if you lived here."

An unfamiliar taste coated Bryce's mouth. Guilt, perhaps? He'd attended college at the University of Washington and decided to stay after graduation. He hadn't always flown back to Philadelphia for the holidays, either. Or vacations. "My life—my business—is in Seattle."

"You can design buildings anywhere."

"You can do construction work anywhere."

They'd had this discussion before and reached an impasse, but that was before his father's fall. Bryce wouldn't let it go this time. He couldn't. He had to convince his dad to leave Marietta. That would be best…for both of them.

"There's plenty of opportunity where I live. People are always remodeling. I know subcontractors and crews. If I get awarded this new project, I'm going to need more help," Bryce added. "Why not try Seattle for a season or two?"

"I don't want to move. I like this town." His dad stared at a framed photo of Bryce's mother sitting on the mantel. "Marietta was your mother's favorite place to visit. She dreamed of moving here someday, so I did it for her."

Bryce felt a pang. If only his mom hadn't kept quiet about not feeling well, but she hadn't wanted to worry anyone. Typical of her, but by the time his father realized how sick she was, there hadn't been much time left. Bryce had flown to his hometown to be with his parents, and his mom died soon after.

Not going to happen with his dad.

Bryce couldn't let sentimentality imprison his father in Marietta. Compromise was an option, too. "You said the past winter was worse than the year before. You could live here during the summer months when the weather is better and spend the rest of the year with me in Seattle."

"In the rain." Disdain laced each of his father's word.

"It doesn't rain every day."

"Almost every day." His father rubbed his chin. Even with broken legs, his dad shaved each morning because his mom had preferred that. "You'd get tired of having me around."

"Never."

"See how you feel at the end of the month. You said the town was quaint. You might like Marietta better by then and want to move here."

No way would that happen, but Bryce wouldn't say that aloud. "Who knows?"

Even though he did.

The sooner he could get his dad out of the western-themed Podunk town full of men who wore Wrangler jeans and cowboy boots and women who chased the same men based on the size of their shiny belt buckles, the better.

Though he recognized a little bit of the small-town appeal. People acted friendly and were always smiling.

Especially the ones who worked in the stores. Speaking of which…

"Want some of that chocolate I bought?" Bryce asked.

"It's not for me. I had you buy my friends' favorites, so I can give it to them when they come over."

"That's thoughtful of you." And so unlike his dad, who had often forgotten anniversaries and birthdays due to being busy on a job site. His mother's death had devastated his father, but moving to Marietta three years ago had changed him.

"You've seen the amount of food they've brought over for us. That's the least I could do."

"True." The food was delicious and surprisingly healthy for small-town cooks without access to gourmet or organic grocery stores. "Need anything right now?"

"Nope." His dad touched Bryce's arm. "I'm just happy you're here."

The cement roller driving across his chest made him struggle for a breath. "Me, too."

A knock sounded on the door.

"Another one of your female friends delivering dinner?" Bryce hadn't cooked—other than warming up food—since he'd arrived. The women in town kept his father's fridge full. "Better get that chocolate ready."

"No one texted that they were stopping by."

"Maybe one of your female admirers wants to surprise you."

"Not admirers, just friends."

"So you keep saying." Bryce hoped his dad was telling the truth. The fewer attachments he had in Marietta, the easier moving him to Seattle would be. "Better see who it is."

"If it's a kid trying to raise money for school, buy whatever they're selling."

"You act gruff and tough, but you're just a big softie."

"Nah. I'm still a mean SOB. I just have more disposable income now, so I can support groups in the community. You don't really think I'm going to eat all those boxes of cookies in the pantry, do you?"

"Then why are there so many empty boxes in the recycle bin?" Without waiting for an answer, Bryce opened the front door.

He expected to see a middle-aged or older woman holding a casserole covered with aluminum foil, not a pretty twenty-something woman with light brown hair and two dogs—a large, part German shepherd mutt and a smaller Pomeranian mix. She looked familiar, but he couldn't place her.

Her eyes widened. "It's you. I mean, you were at the chocolate shop earlier. I work there."

The friendly salesclerk. Except… "You look different."

"No apron."

Bryce didn't remember what she'd been wearing. All he'd wanted to do was get back to his father's house as quickly as he could. "I—"

The larger dog bounded upward, like a stallion rearing, and pushed two front paws against Bryce. The weight sent him back a step. The memory of being chased by a big dog when he was a kid sent a rush of adrenaline through his veins.

He raised his hands to protect himself.

"Off," a woman yelled.

Something licked Bryce's cheek. Cringing, he turned his face away.

The weight against him disappeared.

The dog, either on its own or by force, returned to the woman's side.

Good. Bryce wasn't a fan of big dogs. All they did was get in the way and act menacing. Although, this one stared up at Bryce with what appeared to be a goofy canine smile. Still, the glint in its eyes shouted pure mischief.

"I'm so sorry." The woman shortened the length of the leash on the larger dog. "Rascal is still learning how to act around new people. Are you okay?"

"I'm fine." Bryce wiped the dog slobber off his cheek with the back of his hand. "No thanks to that beast of yours."

"Rascal's a friendly sort of beast." She didn't seem embarrassed by her dog's bad behavior. "We've been working to mend his Sasquatch ways, but canine manners take time. Especially with excitable puppies. On the bright side, he didn't wet on you. That's progress."

If she expected him to laugh or play along, Bryce wouldn't. Though he had to admit that slobber was better than urine.

"By the way, I'm Dakota Parker."

Her easy smile had caught his eye at the chocolate shop, and it was what made him take a second look now.

Warm brown eyes. Clear, smooth skin. French braided light brown hair. She wasn't that tall—the top of her head came up to his nose—but above average height. Pretty. The multi-colored striped scarf around her neck looked hand knitted based on the random color pattern and lopsided lines.

Her baggy gray sweatshirt didn't tell him much about the curves underneath, but the way her jeans hugged her hips hinted at...possibilities. The jeans weren't the skinny type that the fashion-obsessed Chelsea preferred. Definitely not designer ones, either.

Dakota's casual style was surprisingly refreshing. Pouncing, slobbering dog aside. At least the smaller mutt behaved and stayed at her side.

Amusement gleamed in her eyes. "Would you like me to turn around so you can get a better look?"

Her directness was attractive, but he wasn't interested in anyone or anything related to Marietta. Best to shut this down before she got the wrong idea. "No, thanks. I've seen enough."

"Well, then." She sounded like she was trying not to

laugh. "I'd say a handshake should come next, but I don't want Rascal planting another wet one on you or mistaking you for a tree."

Did his pants resemble a tree trunk?

Not wanting to take the chance, Bryce stepped back, though he doubted distance would stop the mutt from doing whatever he wanted. "Appreciate that."

Her gaze softened. "In spite of his behavior, Rascal is a sweet boy."

Was his owner sweet? Best not to think about that. Her. Not when she had a bodyguard dog who probably wouldn't appreciate any man getting close.

Bryce eyed the beast warily. "A sweet boy with pointy, sink-into-flesh teeth."

"As long as you're not wearing Eau de Bacon, you should be fine."

He'd give her points for having a sense of humor. Not that he was keeping score. "Should, not will?"

She grinned. "Well, how am I supposed to know if you're a bacon lover who also moisturizes with cheese fondue? But no worries if you are. I have a tight grip on Rascal's leash. He's not going anywhere, but I think he jumped on you because he likes you."

Bryce didn't quite know what to make of Dakota or her wild dog, but he found himself smiling and enjoying their conversation. "Well, I did have a BLT for lunch."

"That explains it."

His gaze traveled the length of the leash to her hand. He didn't think selling chocolate would be considered manual labor, but her skin looked rough and scarred. Her fingernails were trimmed short and painted navy blue with hot pink polka dots. No bracelets or rings.

Not that he cared if she were married or engaged. She simply piqued his curiosity after only having women older than her visit since he arrived.

"Don't follow Rascal's lead by showing off your bad manners," his father said from his recliner. "Dakota introduced herself. It's your turn."

Heat rose up Bryce's neck. He was being rude, but being chastised by his dad was worse. "I'm Bryce Grayson."

"My son from Seattle," his dad added, as if having the same last name wasn't enough for Dakota.

She nodded. "I see the resemblance now."

"Bryce inherited his good looks from me. The rest comes from his mother. Thank goodness."

For years, Bryce's mom had called herself a DNA copy machine, but as he'd gotten older, she'd taken solace in knowing much of his personality and design talent came from her. Though she claimed he was as stubborn as his father.

Bryce wasn't.

"Since my son doesn't seem to be in any hurry to invite you in, I will. Please, come inside." His father motioned to Dakota. "The dogs are welcome, too."

Say what? The man in the recliner looked like his dad, but he wasn't acting like him. No animals had been inside his parents' house since Spartacus, the family's thirteen-year-old pug. His death had broken his parents' hearts. Bryce's, too.

The dog had been the only one that Bryce liked being around.

Spartacus didn't chase, growl, or bite. He was so smart, loving, and the perfect size, unlike the monster that had just pounced on him.

After losing Spartacus, his parents had said no more animals. Not only no dogs, but also no cats, birds, hamsters, or fish, either. His father had reiterated the point when he moved to Marietta.

Something must have changed. But why these two? The smaller dog seemed okay. The larger one, however, was a disaster waiting to happen.

Still, this was his father's house. Bryce would be able to keep his distance. He opened the door wider and stepped out of the way to let them inside. He didn't want the big dog to run him over.

Dakota remained on the porch. She kept a tight grip on the two leashes. "Thanks for the invite. Scout would be fine indoors, but Rascal's still learning what not to chew."

"Or lick," Bryce muttered.

"Yes, but…" Her intense, under-the-microscope scrutiny suggested she was viewing a specimen she didn't like.

Not that he needed her approval.

Or wanted it.

Still, his muscles tensed. The *Jeopardy* countdown theme played in his head. "What?"

"I don't see any permanent damage," she answered finally.

Germs weren't visible, but this probably wasn't the time to bring up the lack of cleanliness in a dog's mouth. No doubt, her retort would make him regret saying anything. He pressed his lips together.

"Bryce looks better if you ask me," his dad said. "A few more rounds with Rascal, and he might not look like such a city slicker."

Even though Bryce was thirty-two, his father could still make him feel like a shy, insecure twelve-year-old. "Gee thanks, Dad. But in case you forgot, you used to live in Philadelphia."

"The suburbs. Doesn't count." His father's grin spread. "I must say I'm thrilled you didn't show up in town wearing one of those ridiculous, unmanly man buns."

Dakota laughed.

Bryce fought the urge to grimace. He hoped his dad didn't bring up his favorite boxers vs. briefs debate.

"Don't worry about Rascal, Dakota," his father continued as if Bryce wasn't there. "The pup likes getting up close and personal. That's probably because he was on his own when he was so young and prefers having people nearby.

You'll have him behaving in no time, just like you always do."

"I'm trying my best," she said.

Bryce's gaze bounced between the two. They seemed to know each other well. And that bothered him.

Who was Dakota Parker and what did she want with his father?

"You know my dream." Dakota scratched behind the larger dog's ear. The beast looked up at her with a severe case of puppy love.

"A forever home for all the animals," his dad said. "How did Lori like your proposal?"

Dakota lowered her head. "She didn't. I need to rewrite it before she'll take the plan to the board. Not sure I can."

"You can, and you will, for the animals at Whiskers and Paw Pals."

The missing piece clicked into place. Bryce's fingers curled. "You work at the chocolate shop and the animal shelter."

She nodded. "I'm a volunteer adoption coordinator and chief gofer."

His jaw tensed. No wonder she was visiting. She must feel guilty. "You were there when my father fell."

Dakota's smile faltered. A serious expression crossed her face. "I was."

"Good thing I didn't crack open my skull. That would take longer to heal than my legs." His dad knocked on his forehead as if this was a big joke and he hadn't been seriously injured. "Can't wait to get back to work on my project."

The corners of Dakota's mouth curved upward in a soft smile that made her seem like she genuinely cared about his dad. "Which one?"

"I do have a few going."

"Only a few?" she asked with a playful tone.

Bryce's temper spiraled at his father's exchange with this woman.

Dakota might be—okay, she was—attractive, but she was also part of the problem with his father living in Marietta. No one was looking out for his dad.

"Why didn't you stop my dad from climbing the ladder?" Bryce asked.

She flinched. "Excuse me?"

"Bryce," his dad warned in a stern voice.

Okay, maybe Bryce shouldn't have worded his question that way, but still...if the shelter workers had showed as much compassion for his dad's safety as they did for animals' well-being, his father would be able to stand and Bryce would be home in Seattle.

"What kind of projects have you done there?" he asked his dad.

"Exterior and interior improvements. I added a room of dog kennels with access to an outdoor run and various things for the cats."

"Your father's a huge asset to Whiskers and Paw Pals,"

Dakota added. "He's our most recent volunteer of the year."

Bryce scratched his neck in confusion. "I thought you'd been hired to do a job there."

"I volunteer, too."

He tried to make sense of what he was hearing. Tried and failed. His dad had never volunteered in Philadelphia. When he worked, he got paid. If his father wasn't working, he was at home. "You volunteer?"

"You betcha."

His father sounded so pleased. Had he forgotten about the two broken legs under the blanket?

"How long have you been doing this?" Bryce asked.

"About a year and a half. Love the people and the animals."

Dakota's smile widened. "We love you, Walt."

This made no sense. Unless…

His dad must be lonely.

Loneliness would explain working for free at a shelter filled with animals that no one wanted when he could get paid doing similar things for clients.

Moving to Seattle was the best option for his dad. No doubt. "Why didn't you tell me what you were doing?"

His dad shrugged. "It's no big deal. Just something I do in my free time."

"Something you do very well," Dakota said. "You've got the place looking so much better."

"Wait until I can do more," his dad said.

"I can't wait to see what you have planned, but having you back on your feet is all that matters right now. You need to rest and heal."

Dakota sounded sensible, but she rubbed Bryce the wrong way. A woman her age should be at happy hour or out on a date, not walking dogs in the cold and visiting old men. Could she be after his father's money?

The larger dog pulled against the leash. Her knuckles turned white.

No wonder she had such a firm handshake and rough hands. She must lift weights to have enough strength to control the beasts she worked with.

"Rascal's restless, but before I go…" Dakota reached into her hoodie's front pocket with the hand holding onto the smaller dog's leash. She handed Bryce a bag. "These are for Walt, but there's enough for him to share."

Bryce didn't want any. Still, bringing something for his father was a nice gesture. Unless she had an ulterior motive behind her friendliness. "Thanks. My dad plans on giving away the chocolate I bought earlier. Now he has some for himself."

"Typical Walt," she said. "He brings in cupcakes or donuts whenever someone's celebrating a birthday."

Interesting. Bryce had never seen that side of his father. His mother had taken care of holidays at their house.

Dakota gripped the large dog's leash tighter. "He's so kind and keeps us from getting into trouble."

"Don't listen to her," his dad said, using his fatherly tone. "Dakota is the one who watches out for everyone. Humans and animals. She's the definition of caring and nice."

"Aw, thanks, but I bet you say that about everyone who visits," she teased.

He didn't. But Bryce wasn't going to say that aloud. Something about her left him feeling...off-kilter. But he didn't know why. He wanted her to leave.

His father laughed. "Only the ones who bring chocolate."

She tilted her head. "I'll remember that for the next time."

"Please do." Hope filled his father's eyes. "You're always welcome."

Bryce's jaw tensed. He had a feeling his dad was more interested in Dakota visiting than her bringing over chocolate. Were they friends or was something else going on? The hair on the back of his neck stiffened.

"I heard Gladys has been by and some of the other blue-jacket ladies, too," Dakota said.

"They need me back on my feet so I can change light-bulbs and get their houses prepped for winter, but Bryce can always do that before he leaves."

Bryce nodded, but he was confused as well as concerned.

Back home, his parents were friendly but kept to themselves outside of work and attending church. Their circle of friends was close but small. Here in Marietta, his dad seemed to be an integral part of the community and have more friends than Bryce could count. Two things that had never seemed important to his dad before moving here.

Once again, loneliness would explain that. Surely, his dad would see moving to Seattle was the best option for him. Bryce had a spare bedroom in his condo. If his proposal was accepted, his design firm would take off. He would be able to buy a house with a big yard or even land. They could build a place in the back if his dad wanted his own space.

The song "Who Let the Dogs Out" played. The music seemed to be coming from behind Dakota.

"Excuse me. That's the rescue's ringtone. They wouldn't call at this hour unless it's important." She pulled her cell phone from her back pocket and held it to her ear. "This is Dakota."

Her face paled. "What?"

Lines creased her forehead. Her shoulders sagged.

The distraught look on her face made Bryce want to reach out to her, but he didn't know how the dog would react, so he kept his arm at his side.

"I'm walking the dogs." Dakota sounded stressed. "I'll take them home and then head over… Yes, I have extra crates in the garage… Okay, see you soon."

She disconnected from the call. "A pipe burst at the shelter. They've called a plumber and the insurance agent. Water is on both floors, and it sounds bad."

His dad straightened as if he were getting ready to stand. "Let's go."

Bryce rushed to the recliner. "You can't go anywhere."

His father frowned. "There's a brief time frame before mold will start to grow. Furniture and other items will need to be cleared out. The animals, too. I have a wheelchair."

"Yes, you do," Dakota said before Bryce could answer. "But you need to heal. That's the most important thing you can do. I have a feeling we're going to need you more than ever."

"Okay, but you need help." His father gave Bryce a look. "Go with her."

He flinched. "Me?"

"You understand buildings. You know how water can compromise a structure. You can help them. Make sure whoever shows up is doing what needs to be done. Drive my truck in case tools are required."

What his father said made sense, but one thing stopped Bryce from agreeing. "I'd go, but I don't want to leave you alone."

His dad picked up his cell phone. "I'll find someone to come over."

Nothing would stop Walt Grayson once he made up his mind. That was the kind of man he was, and had always been.

Bryce had no doubt one of his dad's many female friends would love to help out. They offered daily to come over if

Bryce wanted time to himself.

If he went to the shelter, his father wouldn't feel the need to get involved himself. At least, not tonight. "Okay, I'll go."

Dakota shifted her weight from foot to foot. The dogs pawed at the porch. "I have to get home."

"Don't worry, Dakota," his father said. "Even though we don't always know why, things happen for a reason."

Her nod contradicted her concerned gaze. She looked at Bryce. "You might want to change out of your nice clothes and into something you don't mind getting dirty. Sounds like we'll be walking into a wet mess."

With that, she turned and hurried down the porch steps with the two dogs.

Bryce closed the front door. She'd said his clothes were nice, but he didn't think she meant that as a compliment.

"Anything I should know about the building?" Bryce asked.

"It's a two-story residence that was converted for commercial use. The rescue hasn't been there long. The building is old and in need of updating. I've been doing what I can, but the rescue's had budget issues."

"Is that why you volunteer? To save them money?"

"I have skills that can be put to use, and it gives me something to do between jobs, but I volunteer because I enjoy spending time with good people who love animals," his father said. "The rescue has insurance. The agent is local. But who knows what they'll find if they open the walls or the ceiling due to water damage. Given the age of the building, there could be asbestos. Do what you can to help."

This seemed important to his dad. Maybe if Bryce helped out with this emergency tonight and then finished whatever projects had been started at the rescue, his father would be more willing to move to Seattle. "I will."

"This will be hard on Dakota. She loves those animals. Keep an eye on her."

That was an odd request. "She's old enough to take care of herself."

"Yes, she turned twenty-eight on her last birthday, but in Marietta, we look out for each other. Especially with those who don't have any family around."

Those like Dakota and his father.

One more reason why his dad needed to move to Seattle. Bryce would look after him better than a bunch of strangers.

Especially one whose smile tempted him to grin back in spite of her misbehaving dog.

Chapter Three

NOW THAT THE sun had set, Dakota stood in the Whiskers and Paw Pals parking lot with only one dim lamppost and car headlights to illuminate the area. People kept arriving to help, so many she couldn't keep track of who was who. A few volunteers helped prepare the animals for transport. Some filled white plastic trash bags with food and information sheets for each animal. Others placed the bags next to the appropriate crates.

Dakota stood nearby with her cell phone in hand. She phoned vet clinics, rescue groups, fosters, and friends to try to locate temporary housing for the animals and crates they could borrow for transport. She spoke over the barks and meows—not unusual sounds at the rescue—coming from the rows of crates already filled.

The goal was to clear the rescue and transport the animals in an organized fashion, but she couldn't stop wondering what was going on inside the building. Bryce might know. He was here. Somewhere.

Walt's truck was parked next to the plumber's van, but

she hadn't seen Bryce. Maybe he'd taken her advice and changed clothes. She might not recognize him in casual attire. Strike that. Wearing grubbies wouldn't change his looks.

His gorgeous eyes appeared front and center in her mind.

Not what she should be thinking about after he'd stared at her as if she were a piece of moldy bread at Walt's house. When Bryce had figured out she volunteered at the rescue…

Her muscles tensed.

The accusation in his voice cut deep. As if she or anyone else at the rescue would do anything to hurt Walt.

Whatever.

Physical attractiveness said nothing about a person's insides. She knew better than to be charmed by a pretty face and sweet words.

Been there, done that. Never again.

She'd believed her ex-fiancé Craig when he said he wanted to spend the rest of their lives together. She'd planned a wedding, bought a dress, and thought they'd love each other forever.

Yeah, right.

He'd lied.

She doubted he'd ever loved her.

Dakota rolled her shoulders to loosen her tight muscles. She needed to concentrate on her work here. If all went according to plan, the rescue would have no animals inside when the doors were locked tonight.

"Be careful what you wish for," she muttered.

"I beg your pardon?" Veronica Keller asked. She was one of the volunteers who'd shown up tonight to help. Twice a week, she walked dogs at the rescue. She also worked as a receptionist at the Copper Mountain Animal Hospital.

"Just talking to myself."

Dakota dreamed of having every kennel and crate at the rescue empty, but a broken water pipe wasn't how she saw that happening.

Veronica attached strips of masking tape to the tops of crates and then wrote the name of the animal inside. "How are the calls going?"

"Good." Dakota tucked her phone in her back pocket. "Between those and a social media blast, we have temporary foster offers stretching from Bozeman to Livingston, including several here in Marietta. We need a few more."

A total of sixty-five spots were needed—twenty-one dogs and forty-two cats, along with two rabbits that had arrived earlier today and hadn't yet been vetted. Not quite full capacity, but close.

"I'm waiting to hear back from a few people, and then I'll make more calls," she added.

Everything appeared to be going well so far, but Dakota worried she might be forgetting something important. "I want to double-check that each animal has an info sheet."

The pages came from a three-ring binder that could be accessed in a hurry. No printer required in case of power outage. One copy belonged to the rescue. The other would go with the animal.

Veronica raised the roll of tape. "I'll get back to taping the crates."

Dakota walked to the end of one row. Her feet ached after standing all day at the chocolate shop, but she wasn't about to take a break until the animals were on their way.

Inside the first crate, a yellow Labrador puppy named Frisco slept in spite of the noise. A paw twitched. He must be dreaming.

That thought brought a much-needed smile to her face.

Dakota made sure the puppy's name was written on the info sheet. She didn't read the rest of the page. One word was enough for her tired brain to process. She placed the paper back into the bag and moved onto the next animal.

"Hungry?"

She jumped. The male voice startled her.

Bryce Grayson stood off to the side. He looked like he didn't want to get too close to the dogs even though they were in crates.

The man was hot—no denying that—but not even his eyes could compare to the pizza box he held. That was the most attractive thing she'd seen in hours.

Her stomach did a happy dance.

"Starving," she answered. "I skipped lunch and was planning to eat dinner after I walked the dogs."

"Someone ordered pizza. We've been chowing down on

the other side of the parking lot, but I wanted to make sure you and the people over here got slices."

That was thoughtful of him. Unexpected given his attitude when he'd talked to her at Walt's place. "Thanks."

Was Bryce more like his father than not? So far, she hadn't seen that many similarities between the two beyond their gender and looks. The way Bryce had flinched around Rascal made her wonder if he was either scared of dogs or didn't like them. Maybe both?

He brought the box closer. "I hope you like pepperoni."

As he opened the lid, she wanted to sigh. The smell greeted her like a long lost friend. "My favorite."

"Take a slice."

She didn't have to be told twice. She took a piece and a napkin tucked inside the box. "Still warm. Nice job."

A charming smile that heated her insides was his reply.

Better eat before she said something to him she might regret. Dakota bit into the piece.

The seasoning, sauce, and pepperoni exploded in her mouth. The cheese was gooey. Just the way she liked it. She savored the taste and then swallowed.

"This is exactly what I needed." She took bite after bite until the piece disappeared.

He offered the box again. "Have another slice."

She counted the number of people working around the crates. "Give everyone else a piece first."

"Sure?"

"Positive." She wiped her mouth with the napkin. "I didn't expect to eat anything until I got home. This is all I need for now."

With her stomach satisfied, Dakota noticed Bryce had changed out of the loafers and into work boots. Black ones tied with laces.

Smart move, but he hadn't changed his clothes. Stains, a combination of water and mud, streaked his khaki pants.

Should have listened to me.

Kelly had told Dakota she couldn't help everyone, but she still had to try. However, what Bryce wore or did to his clothing was none of her business.

"Thanks again for the pizza." She hoped he took the hint and left her alone.

"You have a lot to do."

"Transferring a rescue full of animals is not an easy task. No one could do it alone, but fortunately, there's plenty of help." She tilted her head toward the volunteers and staff working around her. "I appreciate them, and I'm also thankful you're helping out."

"I haven't done much."

She took another look at him. "You're pretty dirty for standing around."

"I've been moving items out. Not working hard like you."

The hair on her arms prickled. She eyed him warily. "You've been watching me?"

"My dad asked me to keep an eye out for you."

That sounded like Walt. Dakota guessed he ordered the pizzas, too. She could take care of herself, but she wouldn't say anything that might hurt Walt's feelings. "Tell your dad I'm doing great."

"You must be tired after working at your other job."

Complaining wouldn't help the animals, and it would only aggravate her. "Others here worked longer hours than me. They have to be more tired and hungry."

"I'll pass out the pizza before it gets cold."

Before she could thank him, he was walking toward Veronica.

Dakota read the name on the next info sheet and jotted a note about Casper liking warm water mixed in his food. She read the sentence twice, corrected two spelling mistakes, and slipped the page into the bag.

Her gaze, however, followed Bryce.

Stop.

Yes, he was attractive.

But this wasn't the time or place to be staring at him.

A Patterdale Terrier named Bodie pawed at the door to his crate. He'd been found on the side of the highway over a month ago. No collar or microchip, but he could sit, shake, and roll over on command. Unfortunately, no one responded to the lost and found posts on the Internet or in the Copper Mountain Courier.

"You'll be able to run around soon," she said.

The dog stared up at her as if he understood.

She had no doubt he did.

She caught a glimpse of Bryce passing out more pizza. Making sure they ate was a nice gesture.

"Dakota!"

Maddie Cash, an agent with Styles Realty, wove her way around the crates. She was stunning with long, blond hair and expertly applied makeup. Her A-line yellow wool coat was buttoned at the top, but swung open at the bottom and showed off multicolored print leggings tucked into stylish black boots, a fashionable tunic, and a sparkly necklace.

"I heard about the broken pipe and came right over." Concerned filled Maddie's voice. She touched Dakota's arm. "Is there anything I can do to help?"

At first glance, the real estate agent appeared to be nothing more than a party girl who used her daddy's credit card to color her supermodel hair and buy fashionista clothing, but beneath the glitz and glam was a generous young woman with a warm heart. Dakota had gotten to know Maddie at one of the rescue's fundraising events where the real estate agent had surprisingly mentioned wanting to foster a dog.

No time like the present.

"Is there any way you could take one of the dogs temporarily?" Dakota asked. "I need to find places for all of them, so if you could take one for tonight—"

"Tonight or longer. Whatever you need." The words rushed from Maddie's mouth. "I read the info you gave me on fostering. I'm happy to help. I would love to help."

"Thank you." Dakota studied the list of dogs to see who would fit best with Maddie. "Clementine."

"Excuse me?"

"We have a young Yorkshire Terrier mix named Clementine who, I think, will be perfect for you and you for her. Clementine's elderly owner passed away recently, and the dog was surrendered to the rescue by the woman's family."

"How sad."

Dakota nodded. "Animals grieve, too. Being in a home instead of at another rescue group or vet office will be better for Clementine. She's a sweet pup, but she does have a bit of an attitude. I'm not sure I'd call her a diva, but I believe she might have been a tad indulged in her former home."

Maddie grinned. "Clementine and I should get along splendidly."

"I'll warn you that she needs training. Obedience isn't in her vocabulary yet. She also tinkles if she gets too excited."

"No problem. It's only for a few days." Maddie didn't hesitate, which lessened Dakota's concerns. "I have hardwood floors. That will make any cleanup easy."

"Fantastic." Dakota handed her clipboard to Maddie. A pen was attached with a frayed string. "Fill out this form while I get her."

She walked toward the smaller crates and then picked up Clementine's along with her bag. "You, my beautiful girl, just hit the lottery. I bet you find yourself with a blinged-out collar. Hot pink or purple would be my guess. And a matching sweater. Designer label."

Clementine lifted her nose as if she were above humans. Well, Dakota.

"Be nice," she said. "You might be able to turn this into a permanent gig."

The dog looked away.

"Suit yourself." A minute later, she handed the crate and plastic bag to Maddie. "This is Clementine."

Maddie peered into the crate. "Hello, little one. You're as pretty as a princess. Bet you'd look adorable in a tiny tiara."

Clementine barked.

"Is that a good sign?" Maddie asked.

"Yes." Considering the real estate agent received a reply from the dog while Dakota had been ignored completely. "A very good sign."

Maddie blew out a puff of air.

Dakota scanned the filled-out form. "Everything looks good. Inside the bag is information about Clementine and food."

Maddie beamed "I'm—we're—all set."

"I really appreciate this."

Maddie glanced at the crate in one hand and the trash bag in the other. Her smile wavered before widening. "I'm glad I could help."

"I'll let you know when the animals can return to the rescue, and please call me if you have any questions. My number is on the info sheet."

"I will. And if you need any places for cats, contact Cynthia Henley. She's my stepsister and is a crazy cat-lover."

With that, Maddie walked off with Clementine.

One less dog to place tonight…

Dakota wrote Cynthia's name down on the potential cat foster list.

The barks and meows increased. Dakota had no idea why, but the cacophony of confusion, disapproval, and fear broke her heart. Who wanted to find themselves in unfamiliar crates outside at night? Being at the rescue was hard enough for some.

"It's going to be okay." She said the words to no dog or cat in particular, and as much for the animals as herself. She wanted to stay positive, but uncertainty was increasing by the minute.

If only she knew more about the water damage inside…

Worry knotted her stomach.

"I've got two more for you." Dustin Decker, a wrangler with all-American good looks who worked at the Bar V5 Dude Ranch, held onto the leash of a bulldog named Dozer and a smaller cat carrier containing a calico named Patches. "The dog is wet. He decided to play in the puddles on our way out."

"Oh, Dozer. You water dog, you." She set her clipboard on a crate and picked up a nearby towel. "Let's get you dried off."

The cowboy walked with a slight limp due to old rodeo injuries. He handed her Dozer's leash and set the cat crate near the other felines.

"A few dogs don't want to wade through the water, so we might have to carry them."

She knew who one might be. "River Jack?"

Dustin's brows drew together. "How did you know?"

"Sounds like him." River Jack was an obese Golden Retriever who'd been found down by the river over a year ago. He was one of the Lonely Hearts—what the staff called the animals that had been at the rescue for months, some even years. "He's been on a diet since he arrived, but he has more weight to lose. Be careful if you try to lift him."

"Doubt River Jack's heavier than the calves I work with." Dustin flashed her a charming grin. "I can handle him."

"Promise me you'll bend your knees."

He tipped his hat. "I promise."

As Dustin walked back toward the building, she toweled off Dozer.

Gratitude swelled inside her for Dustin and the others who had shown up due to a callout made at Grey's Saloon. Dakota wasn't surprised so many people had come to help. The caring community was one of the big draws of this quaint, small town.

An army brat, she'd moved so much growing up that she didn't feel like she'd ever had a hometown, just a long list of places where she'd lived. Whenever she'd visited her great aunt Alice, who lived in Marietta, she'd felt different, as if she belonged here. When her aging aunt had wanted someone to live in the house with her, Dakota, fresh from college with a hard-earned sociology degree, had jumped at the opportunity. She could "put down roots" as Aunt Alice used to say. And Dakota had. She planned to stay forever and hoped to convince her brother York to move here after he left the Air Force in the spring.

Dakota might not be as smart as her siblings, but she could make a home for her brother and sister. A place they could come to for a vacation or permanently, but not like the base housing or rentals they'd lived in growing up. No worries about pets being allowed or the security deposit not being returned. A house that was fully paid for thanks to the generosity of Aunt Alice who'd left her entire estate to Dakota.

"You're drier now." She patted Dozer's head. "Let's put you into a crate where you'll be safe."

The dog trotted into an empty crate.

"Good boy." She locked the door and double-checked the latch was secure. "I'll be back to check on you."

Amid the barks and meows, a whimpering sounded.

Oh, no. Someone was unhappy. Most likely afraid due to their new surroundings. She needed to find out who ASAP.

Clipboard in hand, Dakota followed the sound. The whimpers grew louder. She was getting closer, but she noticed none of the dogs near her looked happy.

Molly, a poodle mix, faced the back of the crate as if in a time out, but she wasn't making a sound. She was a lap dog who loved being petted and brushed. The dog hadn't gotten along with her owner's new boyfriend, so Molly had been surrendered. A generous donation had been made for the dog's care, but that hadn't helped the dog understand why she'd been left.

"You'll be inside soon. I promise."

Molly didn't move. The only time she perked up was when someone held her.

Poor baby.

If Dakota had been faced with the same decision, she would have dumped the guy and kept Molly. Dogs were the best judge of character. None of her foster dogs had liked Craig or her other ex-boyfriends, either. The men had blamed the animals and the rescue for taking too much of her time. She would have to remember to trust the animals' judgment the next time she dated.

The whimpering stopped.

That didn't mean all was well. She needed to find the dog.

The next crate contained Fred, who'd come to them from a high-kill shelter in Southern California. The Dachshund mix trembled, even though he wore a sweater that a volunteer had knitted for him. Fred was another Lonely Heart animal. He'd lived at the rescue for over a year.

"You look dapper, Fred, but it's colder than you're used

to. You won't be outside much longer."

The whimpering sounded again.

Who was that?

She spotted the crate—Maverick, a Border collie whose owner, a retired rancher from Livingston, had entered an assisted living center two weeks ago. Pets weren't allowed in the facility. With no other family around, Maverick had no place to go, so he'd ended up at Whiskers and Paw Pals.

She kneeled in front of the crate's door.

Maverick's head hung low. Being in the rescue was hard enough after having a huge ranch to roam. She had no doubt he hated being locked in this hard-sided crate.

Dakota stuck her fingers through the door's grate. "I can't let you out, honey. This is the safest place for you right now." She touched his fur with her fingertips. "You're going to spend tonight somewhere else. Maybe tomorrow, too, but you'll be back before you know it. If not, I'll come visit. I promise."

Maverick rubbed his muzzle against her fingers.

Her heart squeezed. The dog was seven, well behaved, and loved kids and cats. Dakota was surprised he was still at the rescue, but adoptions had been slow lately, which was why they were so full.

"You're such a good boy." Touching Maverick seemed to calm him. "You'll find a new home soon."

Maverick's ears perked.

"What is it?"

"The dog likes you," Bryce said. She recognized his voice this time.

"This is Maverick." She kept her fingers between the grating. "He likes everyone."

Too bad she couldn't say the same about Bryce. Okay, that wasn't nice. The man had brought her pizza.

Dakota focused her attention on Maverick, who pressed against her fingers. He wanted to be on her lap, but she couldn't let him out. Instead, she petted him as best she could.

"There's pizza left," Bryce said.

She glanced over her shoulder. Her gaze stared right at his pant zipper. She gulped. Not the view she expected or wanted.

Dakota faced the dog.

Maverick pressed his wet nose against her fingers.

She leaned closer to the crate and whispered, "Be right back."

Dakota stood. "Thanks, but one slice was enough."

Bryce gave the dog a cursory glance—one that matched his eye roll when Walt had talked about volunteering at the rescue.

Whether he liked animals or not was unimportant. He was here. Sure, his father had told him to come, but Bryce had construction knowledge. Maybe he knew the status of the building.

"How bad is the damage inside?" She asked the question

that had been weighing on her mind and her heart.

Bryce didn't say anything.

"That bad?" she asked.

He rubbed his chin. "A major pipe broke and affected both floors. We don't know the extent of the water damage yet, but if this hadn't been discovered until the morning, it would have been much worse."

"A volunteer had stopped by to give animals their medications and clean." Dakota glanced at the building. "Seems like a lot of activity inside."

He nodded. "The water and electricity have been shut off, and plumbers have been draining the pipes while furniture and other things are being moved out of the affected rooms. The insurance agent stopped by, too."

"One of the blessings of living in a small town."

"The rescue's director, Lori, said mold can affect an animal's health so a professional water restoration company has been called in. They'll work through the night. We'll have a better idea of the damage tomorrow."

"Will the animals be able to return then?"

"No."

The one word brought Dakota's worst fears to life. A tennis-ball-sized lump of panic lodged in her throat. She swallowed. That didn't help. "They'll be able to return, right?"

"I hope so."

She crossed her arms over her chest, as if that could protect her, the animals, and the building. "You don't sound hopeful."

"It's hard to say what will happen. The inside is a real mess." His words increased her worry. "Tomorrow, we meet with the claims adjustor."

"We?"

"Since my father can't be here, I've offered to help in his place. Lori asked me to attend the meeting and walk-thru. Though she seems capable enough to handle things herself."

"Lori is. I call her a pet-saving superhero." The director spoke what was on her mind, but she would do anything to help any animal, whether they were part of her group or not. "The rescue is her life, but she knows to ask for help when she needs it."

"Happy to do whatever I can."

Was he? Dakota wanted to believe him, but trusting was hard for her. Especially someone she had just met.

Maverick whimpered, and she stuck her fingers through the grate again. He quieted.

People with headlamps walked into the shelter.

That made her wonder...hope... "If the electricity's off, maybe the inside isn't as bad as it appears tonight. Things could look better in the daylight."

"That's one way to look at the situation." His tone suggested he thought it was the wrong way.

She raised her chin. "What can I say? I'm an optimist."

"I consider myself a realist because I know better than to

get my hopes up."

"You're nothing like your father."

Bryce didn't appear offended. "My father used to be like me, but since moving to Marietta, he's different. He's more like you now. That must be why the two of you get along."

"That's one reason." Walt accepted her as she was, acknowledged her successes even if they weren't changing the world, and he didn't compare her simpler life to that of her higher-achieving siblings. She loved her parents, but her mom wanted Dakota to shoot for loftier goals and her dad thought she should move to a bigger city in spite of owning a house free and clear, having an inheritance that meant she only had to work part time, if that, and loving the town of Marietta. "You're fortunate to have him as a father."

"I am." Bryce straightened. "So what's your interest in my father?"

The accusation in his tone made her wince. He sounded like he had at Walt's house earlier. "Excuse me?"

"The two of you seem close in spite of your age difference."

The innuendo in his words made her cringe. "If you're trying to make a joke, it's not funny."

"I'm not."

Her muscles tensed. "I'm not looking for a sugar daddy if that's what you're implying. Your father and I are close. We're friends. Good ones. He's my go-to guy for advice, too. Nothing more."

Doubt filled Bryce's gaze.

Unbelievable. But she wasn't going to waste her time trying to convince him. She had done nothing wrong.

A white van pulled into the parking lot. Janie O'Brien, head of the Bozeman Animal Sanctuary, had arrived.

Thank goodness. Not only did Janie have impeccable timing, so Dakota could get rid of Bryce, but more animals would be on their way soon.

"Another rescue just arrived." Aunt Alice had worked with Janie's rescue group six years ago when Dakota moved to Marietta. That had been her first taste of animal rescue, and she'd been hooked. Her life had never been the same since. "I need to get the animals loaded."

"I'll help."

Her instinct was to say no. The guy was a jerk. But practicality won out over emotion. The more help she had, the faster she could get the animals into the van and on their way.

"You're not needed inside?" she asked.

"No. We're waiting for the restoration company to arrive. I have time to lift a few crates."

And deliver pizza.

She glanced at the clipboard on Maverick's crate and counted the names. "How about nine?"

Bryce flexed his arms like a weightlifter. "Nine is easy. Now if it were ninety, I might need a little help."

His playfulness was unexpected. That didn't make her

like him any better. Still, she had to say something. "Only a little?"

"If I admit I'd need a lot of help, they might take away my man card." He sounded serious until he smiled.

His charming grin warmed her insides better than a cup of Sage's hot chocolate. Tingles erupted. Nerve endings twitched in anticipation.

Uh-oh. A jerk should not make her feel this way.

Bryce Grayson was trouble. He needed to have the words '*danger—stay away*' tattooed on his face.

Twice, he'd said rude things, yet her body betrayed logic and reacted in spite of her shutting that part off over a year ago.

How had the switch moved back to the on position?

Yes, she'd missed those feelings, but she'd been in self-preservation and survival mode. Chocolate and animals had been enough to fill what was missing, but maybe she was ready for…more.

Not with Bryce.

He'd accused her of hurting Walt and wanting his money.

That was rude and unacceptable.

Being a nice piece of eye candy couldn't make up for his awful personality. Dakota didn't know the man well, but she had no doubt Bryce Grayson was the definition of Mr. Wrong. He might be Walt's son, but she did not need someone like him in her life.

Chapter Four

THE NEXT MORNING after the meeting at the rescue, Bryce walked along Main Street. In Seattle, the sidewalks would be filled at this time. He wasn't surprised few were out here. He stretched his right arm across his chest. His shoulder and back muscles ached. Not sharp pains, but a haven't-been-used-except-in-the-gym soreness that felt good.

These days, he focused on design work, and although he visited work sites, he did so only to follow a project. He couldn't remember the last time he'd been involved in demolition and had forgotten how satisfying physical labor could be.

But after a restless night of tossing and turning, tiredness dogged Bryce. A visit to the coffee shop for a caffeine fix might help.

Pushing a double stroller with twin toddlers, a woman talked on her cell phone. A brown delivery truck parked at the curb, and a man carried cardboard boxes out the side door. A florist placed orange, red, and yellow flowers into a white bucket outside her shop's front door.

Peaceful and quiet.

The same adjectives his dad had used yesterday.

No sirens blared, no horns honked, no angry drivers cursed out the car window.

But Bryce still didn't get the appeal of small-town life.

His phone rang. He checked the screen to see his dad's name and number.

Concern rocketed through Bryce. He placed the phone to his ear. "You okay, Dad?"

"Not really. Gladys beat me in cribbage. She wants to play Texas Hold'em after she heats up a coffee cake. She's in the kitchen now. She must be planning to cheat and will use food to distract me."

Gladys was one of the many ladies in Marietta who brought over food and kept his dad company as needed. She also volunteered at the hospital. Not your typical card shark. "She could just be a better player than you."

"Or she's a whiz at hiding cards. How'd the meeting go?"

"Not bad." That had been a relief, but getting the repairs done quickly could be an issue. Bryce rubbed the back of his neck. "Lori has a job you can do from your recliner."

The director wanted the water damage repaired in days, not weeks. That would depend on the availability of materials and workers. His father's crew was committed to two projects, but his dad would know who could get the job done right and fast.

"I'll tell you more when I get home." Bryce stopped in

front of the coffee shop. "I'm going to grab a coffee first. Want something?"

"Not coffee. Swing by the chocolate shop and buy two small boxes of chocolates. One for Gladys and one for Willa. I want to thank them for sitting with me last night and today," his father explained. "Dakota will know what they like."

Bryce's stomach clenched. She'd been on his mind. Part of the reason he hadn't slept well. He kept seeing the flash of hurt in her eyes. Hurt he'd caused yesterday at his father's house and also in the parking lot without any proof to justify his questions.

"Bryce?" his dad asked.

"I'm here. I, uh, can do that." Not that Bryce wanted to go to the chocolate shop because he felt bad enough. Seeing her would make him feel worse. "Need anything else?"

"Just my legs to heal." His father hung up.

Gladys must have brought out the coffee cake.

Bryce went inside the café and ordered a coffee to go. His father's words echoed in his head.

She's the definition of caring and nice.

Dakota appeared to put others—animals and humans—ahead of herself. Last night, she'd worn her hair tucked inside a wool beanie and the lopsided knitted scarf wrapped around her neck. She'd also been covered with dog hair, cat fur, and water.

She'd looked silly, if he was being honest, but she hadn't

cared. Nothing had mattered to her except doing her job. One she threw herself into.

Yet, he'd accused her of going after his dad, an older gentleman, like a gold digger.

Way to go, Grayson.

He'd acted like a class-A jerk.

Steel I-beams seemed to press down on his shoulders. He shouldn't have said what he did, but he'd allowed his frustration and anger over his father's broken legs and his wanting to remain in Marietta to build. Bryce had taken out his emotions on Dakota.

Twice.

"Bryce," the barista called.

He grabbed his cup and sipped. Black and strong. The way he liked it. No fancy additions or flavors needed.

He would head over to the chocolate shop to buy what his father needed, and, if Dakota was there, offer her an apology.

The question was—would she accept it?

INSIDE THE CHOCOLATE shop, Dakota surveyed the work she and Portia had done arranging the new products. The ghosts and pumpkins sat in the sales basket. The pilgrim hat and turkey molded chocolates had taken over the choice display spots on the counter, in the window, and between artfully arranged copper boxes on shelves.

Satisfaction flowed through her. She and Portia had done

well, and Sage would be happy when she peeked out from the back. "Only a day late, but November has arrived at Copper Mountain Chocolates."

"Looks great," Portia agreed. "Though Aunt Sage said we'll be preparing for Christmas before Thanksgiving arrives."

Dakota kept forgetting Portia had only joined the staff last month. The young woman caught on quick. "Sage will start making holiday products next week. The molded Christmas trees go on sale first."

"You don't wait until Black Friday?"

"No. The shop will be completely decked out for the holidays the day after Thanksgiving, but we also want to cater to tourists who won't be here in December, so a few Christmas products will be for sale this month."

"Oh, that makes sense."

"You're going to have to prepare yourself for what's coming." Dakota wanted to warn the newbie. "Preparing for the holiday rush is only one part of what we'll be doing. We also need to come up with an event to hold before the end of the month so start brainstorming."

"I can't wait to plan another event. I know Rosie has cut back on her hours to work on her writing, but we can pull something off."

Dakota hoped so. "And don't forget, we open an hour earlier from Black Friday through the twenty-fourth of December. The shop is crazy busy. Much worse than yesterday."

"Busy is good." Portia stared out the window with a wistful gaze. "Keeps me from having too much time to think."

"The time goes by faster." Dakota straightened the chocolate cornucopia display to better meet Sage's exacting standards. She stepped back to double-check. "That's better."

Portia leaned against the counter, wrapping her hands around her stomach.

Dakota noticed her coworker's complexion looked a bit greenish. "Do you feel okay?"

"I...I skipped breakfast. I'll eat something on my break and be fine."

"It's slow. Take your break now."

"Once we're finished." Portia straightened. "I like seeing what little touches you, Rosie, and Sage add to the displays."

"You've been doing them without even noticing. You've caught on so fast. And the things you're doing with social media for the shop are awesome."

"Thanks."

Portia had dropped out of college last month—just weeks into her senior year. She'd rented a room from their other coworker until Rosie got engaged to a sexy cowboy named Brant. Once he and his younger sister moved into Rosie's house, Portia went to live with her Aunt Callen at the Circle C Ranch until she found a place of her own. Now Portia lived in an apartment over the garage at the Bramble

House Bed and Breakfast.

"Are you settled in your new place yet?" Dakota asked.

"Getting there. It's so different from being in college." A wistful look crossed Portia's face. "Though I can't beat working here."

"Best. Job. Ever." Next to working with animals, of course. Dakota would be meeting Lori after work, and she was crossing her fingers to hear good news from the rescue's director. "Chocolate makes everything better."

"It's keeping me going."

Uh-oh. That didn't sound good.

Dakota touched Portia's shoulder. "What's going on?"

"Nothing." Portia raised her chin a notch. "I'm fine."

Not *fine* given her hunched shoulders. Portia hadn't spoken much about leaving college, having to move a couple of times since arriving in Marietta, or the boy she'd been dating. Maybe something else had happened. Or maybe all the changes had caught up to her.

Whatever the reason, Dakota wanted to help.

"Glad to hear you're fine." She used her matter-of-fact voice. The same tone York used whenever he interfered big-brother style in her life. "I thought you might be having boyfriend trouble or something."

"No." The word rushed from Portia's mouth faster than salted caramels disappeared during September's rodeo weekend. "I…Austin and I…we've been off and on. Right now, we're off. Over really."

Breakups hurt. Self-confidence took a beating. At least, Dakota's had. She empathized with the animals who thought they'd found a forever home and family to love them only to be surrendered to the rescue. She wouldn't wish that on anyone. Friends, along with chocolate and her foster animals, had eased the heartache. Time, too.

The least she could do was put a smile back on Portia's face. Dakota had to try. "If that's the case, you qualify to join the Chocolate Is Better Than Men Club, aka CIBTMC."

Portia's nose crinkled. "Huh?"

"The club started out as a joke, but it's become a semi-regular thing with meetings at Grey's Saloon."

"Male bashing sessions?"

"No, but we may raise our glasses in hopes karma visits our ex-boyfriends. The club is for those of us who are tired of dating Mr. Wrongs."

"So you're just waiting for Mr. Right to come along?"

Unfortunately, there seemed to be more Mr. Wrongs than Mr. Rights. She wasn't ready to have her heart trampled on again.

"I'm taking a break from men right now," Dakota admitted. "I'm so busy right now. Maybe after the holidays."

"I can understand that." A thoughtful expression crossed Portia's face. "How many members are in the club?"

"Two at the moment. Me and Kelly Hamilton."

Portia tilted her head. "The vet tech who comes in here for hot chocolate?"

"That's her." Kelly was a great friend who always knew the right thing to stay to Dakota. "Feel free to join us on Thursday at Grey's."

"Thanks. This week doesn't work for me, but maybe next time."

With a smile back on her face, Portia straightened a display of boxes shaped like a pyramid.

Mission accomplished. That pleased Dakota.

She noticed the sample tray was low. Not surprising since everyone loved Sage's single-origin bar.

Dakota broke another chocolate bar into pieces to give to customers.

The bell on the door jingled.

Perfect timing.

"Welcome…" She looked up from the chocolate. Her gaze locked on Bryce's blue eyes. A funny feeling grabbed hold of her stomach. Not queasiness, more like bubbles or…tingles. Weird because she should be red-hot angry with him.

"Welcome to Copper Mountain Chocolates," Portia said, shooting Dakota a what-is-wrong-with-you look.

With a slight shrug to dismiss her reaction, Dakota turned her attention to their customer.

Bryce carried a tall-sized cup with a lid and a sleeve from the Java Café down the street. He wore the same leather jacket as last night, but had on a plaid scarf, brown pants, and shoes. Stylish fall clothes. Dressier and more coordinated than what she was used to seeing on the regulars who came into the shop. But then again, he wasn't from here and designed buildings. Maybe he was into color, too.

She raised the full tray of samples. "Would you like a taste of Sage's single-origin dark chocolate bar? Oh, wait. You don't eat chocolate."

"I don't."

Dakota set the tray on the counter. "What does Walt need for his friends?"

Bryce's mouth slanted in a lopsided grin.

Whatever was happening in her tummy increased. She took a deep breath to calm her out-of-control nerves.

"You're not only a dog whisperer, but you're also a mind reader," he said.

Longing surged through her. "I wish."

That would make life easier and more interesting. She could sort through the wrong guys and know what animals were thinking.

"I used logic, not mind reading," she admitted. "You don't eat chocolate, and Walt couldn't have eaten all he has, so why else would you be here?"

"Logically, I could have my own reason for being here."

"You could." His words hinted at a secret, but he could be teasing her or he could be getting ready to offend her again. "Do I need to put on a bulletproof vest?"

Her gaze locked on his. Not quite a stare down, but close. She had no idea what was going on or why he had such an effect on her. He was Walt's son, but also a stranger from out of town. Not someone she'd be interested in, and she knew he felt the same way about her. Yet, she couldn't look away.

"I'm going into the back." Portia made a beeline for the kitchen.

That was weird. Unless Portia wanted to take her break and eat.

Her leaving diffused the tension in the air. It was time to regain control.

"So what kind of chocolate does your dad want?" Dakota asked.

"Two small boxes of chocolates. One for Willa and the other for Gladys. He said you'd know what they like."

"Milk chocolate salted caramels for Willa and assorted truffles for Gladys," Dakota said without hesitation.

"Impressive."

"Not really. Marietta is a small town. You get to know what the locals prefer."

She grabbed two small boxes. Using tongs, she filled the first one with the salted caramels, but her gaze kept straying to Bryce. Each time, she found him watching her the way he had yesterday.

Her fingers trembled.

A ridiculous reaction to a male customer. Except Bryce wasn't someone who just walked into the store. Was that why she was reacting so strangely around him. Because of

Walt?

No matter the reason, she needed to focus. "How's your day going?"

"Good. I was at the rescue earlier."

The meeting! She held the tongs in midair. "Is the damage as bad as you thought?"

"Surprisingly no. You were correct that things look better in the daylight."

A weight lifted from her shoulders. Now if her hands would stop shaking. "When do repairs start?"

"I don't know yet. Lori wants my dad to help pick a crew."

"Couldn't Walt's company do it? He says he trusts his guys implicitly."

"They have two big projects right now, so no time to take on something like this."

Dakota closed the lid. "Too bad."

"We'll figure it out." He sounded confident, but the dark circles under his eyes told her that he was tired.

"Not what you expected to be doing in Montana."

"No, but I don't mind. This is important to my dad. I have to prepare a proposal I'll be turning in when I get back to Seattle, but the quiet is letting me get lots of work done so I can help."

He might have hurt her feelings yesterday, but he seemed to care about his dad enough to spend time with him, even if he was working. Bet he knew how to put together a proposal that wasn't "simplistic." She filled the second box with truffles.

She had more questions about the actual damage, but Bryce wasn't here for small talk. The sooner he left, the better for her peace of mind.

"There's another reason I came to the shop today," he said.

She didn't look up. "What's that?"

"To see you."

She froze, but managed not to drop the chocolate being held by the tongs. "Because…"

"I owe you an apology for the way I spoke to you yesterday at my father's house and outside the rescue. I let emotion get the best of me in both situations."

His words were unexpected. Dakota set the tongs and chocolate on a nearby platter.

Bryce shook his head. "I was wrong. Rude. Twice. I'm very sorry."

She respected a man who could admit he'd made a mistake. Maybe he was more like Walt than she realized. And holding grudges never solved anything. "Apology accepted. I'm sure it's hard seeing your dad injured. You must worry about him."

Bryce nodded. "I do. I lost my mom four years ago, and until my dad fell, I didn't realize how afraid I am of losing him, too."

His words squeezed her heart. A good thing she was on

the other side of the counter, because all she wanted to do was hug him.

He was being protective of his dad. That didn't make what he'd said right, but she understood better now. The times her dad deployed had been tough on the entire family. There were nights when she'd stay awake to pray for his safe return. She only wished words came easier to her. "He's going to recover."

"Yes, but… My dad doesn't think this fall or his broken legs were any big deal."

So like Walt. That made her smile. "Walt's a strong, proud man, but that doesn't mean he hasn't been affected by the accident. He could be more afraid by his fall than he's letting on and putting on a show for you."

"You think?"

"Yes." She rang up the two boxes, placed each into a bag, added tissue paper to the top, and tied ribbon around each of the handles.

He handed her a credit card.

Reading the name Bryce W. Grayson on his card made her laugh. Figured he wouldn't pay cash once she knew his name. "Do you remember what your dad told me last night before I left?"

"No." Bryce signed the sales slip.

"He said we don't always know why, but things happen for a reason." Walt had been talking about the broken pipe, but the words applied here. "Maybe your father's accident brought you to Marietta for something else. Something—I don't know—more important."

Bryce ran his hand along his jawline. A faraway look appeared in his eyes. "You may be right about that."

He sounded better, which was all that mattered to Dakota. She handed him the two bags. "Do you have time for a hot chocolate?"

A wry grin appeared. Those baby blues of his made her insides feel like melted chocolate. That was the last way she should feel about him. "No, but you don't give up, do you?"

She shrugged.

"Another time," he said.

Dakota doubted he'd ever come in for a cup. Her gaze met his.

Something passed between them. A connection. A feeling.

Heat pulsed through her.

Oh, no. She hoped she didn't turn into a gooey mess.

This was bad.

He picked up the two bags. "Thanks."

"You're welcome." The words sounded hoarse, as if the lump she felt in her throat was real and not some figment of her imagination.

Go, she pleaded silently.

Before she did something crazy.

Like invite him out for a coffee and dessert at the bakery down the street where they served other items besides chocolate.

Why was she thinking that way about him?

He opened the door, and the bell rang.

As soon as Bryce walked out of the shop, Dakota picked up a rag and scrubbed the counter. And scrubbed and scrubbed. She had no idea why, but her mind was reeling from his visit and the way she reacted to him.

"Rub any harder and we may need to replace the countertop." Portia walked in from the back. "For someone who says chocolate is better than men, you sure were checking out that guy."

Dakota's chest tightened. She forced herself to breathe.

Had Bryce noticed? She hoped not.

But he was gone, and Portia was here.

Dakota needed to downplay his effect on her. Her coworker had so much going on—moving into a new place and not feeling well.

She rinsed out the rag. "He has nice eyes."

"So do half the cowboys who come in here. You like *him*."

She stopped. "I only met him yesterday. He also said a couple of rude things to me."

Portia shrugged. "You two seem pretty chummy, which tells me you like him."

"He apologized. I was being nice. I don't know him." Dakota rinsed out the rag. She needed Thursday to arrive ASAP, so Kelly could talk some sense into her.

"Then you have a crush."

"I'm too old for crushes."

"You're never too old for a crush." The color had returned to Portia's face. Whatever had been wrong with her stomach seemed better. "He seems interested in you. Maybe he'll ask you out."

A thrill pulsed through Dakota until reality stopped it cold. "I sure hope not. I'd have to say no."

"Because you're too busy."

She tossed the rag into the bleach water bucket and then washed her hands. "Exactly."

"No other reason?" Portia asked.

Dakota remembered the tears and the pain after Craig had called off the wedding. Her foster animals—a cat and a dog at the time—had been the only things to get her out of bed each morning. Not even work could make her forget how much she'd hurt.

Was she ready to open her heart and risk being hurt again?

Maybe, but not with a city guy with pretty blue eyes who lived two states away and let words fly out of his mouth in frustration. The man was Mr. Wrong in so many ways.

"I don't have time to go on a date. I have animals spread across the three counties. That's my priority right now. Not romance."

Chapter Five

AFTER WORK, DAKOTA sat on her living room couch with Pierre, the Dumbo rat she also fostered, on her shoulder. "Is this some kind of joke?"

"No joke." Lori Donovan sat in the chair on the other side of the coffee table. Scout lay on her lap, and Rascal sat at her feet. Both dogs adored the rescue's director. "If we can find homes for all the animals by Thanksgiving, Whiskers and Paw Pals will receive a six-figure donation. I want you to head the adoption effort."

"That's…" Whatever words Dakota was going to say disappeared. She couldn't believe what she was hearing.

"If anyone can do this, you can." Lori petted the dogs, one with each hand. "What do you say?"

No. That was what Dakota wanted to say. No way could she pull this off in less than a month. She pressed her lips together. Pierre's whiskers tickled her neck. She touched his back.

Had Lori forgotten what she'd said about Dakota "living in a fantasyland with pet unicorns and never-ending rainbows" or had the director bought a ticket to go there?

Dakota took a breath. And another. "You said Christmas was an unrealistic time frame for my *Home for the Holidays* proposal. Thanksgiving is a month sooner. And nothing's been presented to the board of directors yet."

"That was before the water damage. The benefactor feels the money would not only help pay for additional repairs, but it would also allow us to update the building and spur adoptions."

Dakota's jaw tensed. "Adoptions shouldn't be spurred."

"Wrong choice of words." Lori stopped rubbing the dogs. "The animals need homes."

Dakota wanted to make sure she wasn't missing anything. "You said *all* animals."

"That's the benefactor's criteria."

"Then my answer is no. Not all animals can be adopted. We have three senior cats in fospice."

That was what the rescue called foster-hospice situations where animals with terminal illnesses spent their final days, weeks, or months in a loving foster home.

"And what about our four Lonely Hearts? None of them has come close to being adopted since they arrived at the rescue. Another eight dogs and cats are in foster-to-adopt situations. We have agreements with those families." The more Dakota said, the less hopeful she became. "Is the benefactor willing to be flexible about those animals?"

Lines formed around Lori's mouth. She sat back in the

chair. "I don't know."

"If not, we...I...can't do this. I'm just a volunteer. This is crazy." That much was clear to Dakota. "Even if the benefactor is willing to compromise, I'm not sure the rescue should do this. Are you sure the offer is legit?"

"Yes, it's legit. I don't understand why this is crazy." Lori's hard gaze bore into Dakota. "You said your dream is to find forever homes for all animals. Now's your chance. Not only can you do that with the rescue's support, but there's also a huge reward at the end."

Dakota thought about what she wanted to say. "Each animal deserves a family and home, but the right ones. A six-figure carrot dangling overhead can't change our mission. We can't loosen the adoption standards and requirements just to receive a donation.

"We won't." Lori spoke firmly. "No animal will be adopted out to meet a quota, but I'll be honest with you, Whiskers and Paw Pals needs the money to survive."

The words hung in the air. This wasn't what Dakota expected to hear. She knew things had gotten tighter, but she was a volunteer and knew little about the financials other than what money they'd raised at events.

Her pulsed raced faster than Rascal when she'd tried to let him go off-leash at the dog park. She took a breath. It didn't help.

"Survive as in keep the doors open?" she asked.

Lori nodded. "We've been hanging on by our fingernails.

Even without the water damage, I've been trying to rework the budget. The medical balances at the veterinarian clinics we use are out of control. We have a large volunteer base, so downsizing paid staff is on the table."

Those people—her friends—depended on the salaries. And with the holidays coming up…

On the table. Not for certain.

Dakota petted Pierre. She knew each fundraiser mattered, but she'd had no idea things were this bad. "I see why this donation is important, but Whiskers and Paw Pals has an excellent reputation for a reason. You've put what's best for the animals before anything else."

Lori rubbed her palms against the side of her jeans so she didn't disturb Scout. "You're concerns about the donation requirements are valid ones."

That made Dakota sit taller in her chair.

"I'll speak to the benefactor and see if there's room for negotiation," Lori added.

"Thank you."

Rascal used Lori's foot as a pillow. "In the meanwhile, rework your proposal with Thanksgiving as the target date. Have it to me by Friday morning."

Dakota's heart dropped. "Friday morning?"

"Ten o'clock."

"O-kay." Pressure pounded at Dakota's forehead like a jackhammer. Her palms sweated. She didn't want to disappoint Lori, but the idea of rewriting the proposal with such a tight deadline terrified Dakota. She trembled.

"Talk to Tim at the feed store and see if we can hold the drive there," Lori added.

Dakota nodded. Clearing her throat, she fought her rising panic. "If the benefactor's willing to compromise, get it in writing so the requirements are clear."

Lori smiled. "You'd make a good lawyer."

That was what her mother wanted her to be. Her mom had married young and never finished college. She'd put an emphasis on education—high school, college, and graduate school—from the time Dakota and her siblings were little kids. Her mom kept saying it wasn't too late for Dakota to go to law school, but college had been challenging enough. She'd discovered why thanks to a tutor—Dakota had a reading disability that had never been diagnosed—and learned skills so she wouldn't get so frustrated, but the thought of law school still intimidated her. Six years ago, she'd decided not to apply as her mom wanted and moved to live with Aunt Alice in Marietta instead.

"Thanks, but I hate dressing up." Dakota kept her tone light, but her insides twisted from years of feeling inadequate and stupid. "I also doubt they allow anything other than service dogs in the courthouse."

That made Lori smile. She moved a sleeping Scout from her lap and then stood. "I'll be in touch, but, in the meanwhile, rewrite your *Home for the Holidays* proposal with this new time frame. You can fill in the adoption goal once I hear back from the benefactor."

"Who is it?"

"Anonymous. The person approached us through an attorney in Bozeman."

"That's weird."

Lori shrugged. "The wealthy can be eccentric."

Eccentric or not, this didn't sound right to Dakota. "Still seems strange."

Lori laughed. "Yes, it does. I'll call as soon as I know anything more. See you on Friday morning."

The woman gave each dog a pat and Pierre, too, before she headed out the door.

"That was unexpected," she said to the animals. "I wish you guys could talk back and let me know what you think."

Scout slept. Rascal chased his tail. Pierre closed his eyes on her shoulder.

"I suppose if you could talk, we wouldn't need a donation to save the rescue. We would go on TV and get the money ourselves."

But since they couldn't, it meant she needed to rewrite the proposal in a little over a day and a half. Teaching the animals to talk might be easier.

Okay, not really, but that was how impossible the rewrite felt right now.

She glanced at the clock on the wall. Her brother and her sister lived on the East Coast. It wasn't that late, but Dakota needed help they couldn't give long distance.

Who could she ask?

Her coworker Rosie was a professional writer, but she had another television script due and had cut back her shifts at the chocolate shop to only one day a week.

Think.

Kelly had been working extra shifts at the animal hospital due to a virus running rampant. She needed a night at Grey's for a CIBTM meeting, nothing else.

There had to be someone. Dakota rubbed her aching forehead.

Who?

Wait a minute. Walt would know. He always gave the best advice. She grabbed her phone off the table to text him.

Dakota: *Lori just left. Need to talk. Can I come over, please?*

Bryce being at the house shouldn't stop her from going over there. He'd apologized for the things he'd said; she'd accepted his apology. End of story.

So what if she'd been thinking about his smile, his eyes, and the way he'd apologized this afternoon. That didn't mean anything other than, as Portia had said, she might have a crush—an itty-bitty one—on him.

Dakota's cell phone beeped.

Walt: *Not going anywhere. Come over.*

She put Pierre in his cage on the dining room table. "I'll

be back, sweetie."

Pierre had been left in a cage when his family moved out of their house. The new owners had called animal control, who then asked the rescue to take the abandoned rat. Being at the rescue had stressed out Pierre so she'd taken him home with her. He was now thriving at her house, even though she'd never fostered a rat.

The dogs went to their nearby crates. They knew the routine.

Warmth spread through Dakota. She loved these silly dogs.

Scout was almost seven years old and ready for adoption, but Rascal, only nine months old, needed more training. He had more energy than obedience skills, but that could be said of many puppies. He was big, but gentle, with the sweetest disposition.

"Both of you have been so good, and you've been in your crates so much the last few days, I'll let you stay out while I'm gone." She crated them when she wasn't home and when she went to bed. "I won't be long."

Scout curled up on a large dog pillow beneath Pierre's cage. The Pekinese-Pomeranian mix had surprisingly bonded with the Dumbo rat. The two spent as much time together as they could, but Pierre kept his distance from Rascal. That proved he was one smart rat.

The puppy sniffed along the edges of the floor. She had no idea what he smelled since she swept and mopped the floor daily. But who knew what that dog was thinking?

"When I get back, we can play until bedtime."

She blew each a kiss and then pulled the gate across the doorway to the dining room and secured it in place.

Dakota walked to Walt's house, which was two blocks away. Street lamps illuminated the road and sidewalk. The cold nipped at her cheeks so she looped her scarf, knitted by her sister, around her neck another time. Her hands stayed warm in the fleece-lined gloves her brother had given to her for Christmas last year.

Walt's porch light was on, but the curtains were drawn.

She knocked.

Bryce opened the front door. He was wearing the same brown pants as shoes as earlier, but now she saw his long-sleeved plaid shirt.

Handsome if you like the hipster-inspired style. She had to admit Bryce pulled off the look.

"My dad said you were coming over, but that was quick."

"I don't live far."

He motioned her inside. "Please, come in."

As soon as she stepped inside, warmth enveloped her from the combination of forced-air heating and crackling logs in the fireplace. Not wanting to sweat, she removed her jacket, hat, scarf, and gloves.

"I'll take those," Bryce offered.

She appreciated his manners.

The scent of basil and tomatoes hung on the air. Someone must have dropped off an Italian dish for dinner.

Walt sat in his recliner in the living room, so she walked over there.

Bryce's soap-and-water scent tickled her nose. His body heat made the warm temperature in the room rise. He must be right behind her.

Dakota sat on the couch. "Sorry to bother you."

Walt was in his recliner. "It's always good to see you."

"Would you like something to drink?" Bryce asked.

She leaned back against a throw pillow. "No, thanks."

He sat on the couch.

A little too close if she was being honest. Her pulse spurted.

No big deal. There wasn't any other place for him to sit except the floor. Maybe she should move down there.

"What's going on?" Walt asked in that warm tone of his. "You said Lori had just left."

Dakota told them about her conversation with Lori, including the director's comments about the original *Home for the Holidays* plan. "The key to my first proposal was making foster to adopt an official program at the rescue. That gives adopters a trial period to make sure the placement is a good fit for all. The success of the program also hinged on having two months to publicize and hold adoption events. But Thanksgiving is less than a month away."

Walt nodded. "Lori's sending mixed messages."

"Or seeing dollar signs," Bryce said.

"I don't know what to think," Dakota admitted. "Lori said the same adoption standards and approval process would remain in place. She also admitted the shelter is struggling financially."

"How'd you leave it?" Walt asked Dakota.

"Lori said she'd be in touch after she talks to the benefactor's attorney about my concerns."

"At least you didn't have to decide right then," Walt said.

Thank goodness, because Dakota wasn't sure what she would have done.

"I'm worried about staff being laid off and the animals." She rubbed her hands over her face. "I'm not even sure what I want the benefactor to say about the changes we want. I wish this would all just go away and the building would go back to normal."

Bryce reached across the couch and touched her arm. "It'll work out."

His touch was nothing more than a gesture of kindness, but she had to force herself not to scoot closer. She was like some of the dogs at the rescue. She preferred to be part of a pack, not on her own.

"Whiskers and Paw Pals has been struggling financially," Walt said.

"It's the nature of animal rescue." But a dark thought kept surfacing. One that caused an iron grip to squeeze the air out of her lungs. "But what if the benefactor agrees to change the number of adoptions needed? What if I take this on and fail? I'd cause the rescue to close and everyone to be laid off."

Bryce squeezed. "If that happens, and that's a big if, you wouldn't be the one to blame. You are not responsible."

"He's correct." Walt's gaze darkened. "This wouldn't be your fault."

Dakota nodded. She wanted to believe that. "Lori asked me to put together an adoption event for this weekend just in case."

"That sounds like a lot to do given it's Wednesday night," Bryce said.

"I've set up a drive with less time. We have volunteers to help. And whether we're going for the donation or not, the animals deserve loving homes. That's been my priority since I started doing this, and I'll keep trying to find them homes."

"Not trying would be failing. Giving this a shot, no matter the outcome, means you've won." Walt's confidence in her was stronger than her own. "You can do whatever you set your mind to do."

Dakota nodded, not trusting her own voice. She wished she believed that. With so many counting on her, she couldn't afford to make any mistakes, but everything seemed to take her longer to do than everyone else. She was scared she would mess up.

Bryce's hand was still on her arm. She had no idea why,

but his touch comforted.

"Lori also wants me to turn in a revised proposal by ten o'clock on Friday morning," Dakota said.

"The first one took you a long time to write. Can you have the proposal revised by then and plan an adoption event at the same time?" Walt asked.

That was the question of the day. Dakota thought for a moment. "I'm not worried about the event, but I think... No, I'm going to need help with the report. I just don't know who to ask."

Walt rubbed his chin. "I do."

Relief flooded her. The tension in her shoulders loosened. Walt never let her down. "Who?"

"Bryce."

"Me?" he asked.

"You're working on a proposal right now. You have experience."

Dakota remembered what Bryce had said earlier at the chocolate shop.

I have to prepare a proposal I'll be turning in when I get back to Seattle.

But still...Bryce Grayson was the last person she wanted to help her. Few outside her family knew about her reading difficulties. Her mother's reaction and disbelief over the diagnosis had made Dakota not want to tell another soul. Though Dakota had a feeling her closest friends had guessed what was going on.

"A design proposal," he countered.

Walt waved off his concern as if he were swatting a fly. "A proposal is a proposal."

Not in this case, but Dakota didn't want to hurt Walt's feelings. He was only trying to help. "I understand why you're suggesting Bryce, but he's busy with you and his own work. He doesn't have time."

"She's right. I don't," Bryce said.

"We're talking a day's worth of work," Walt countered. "Most likely not even that since Dakota works."

"I don't want to put anyone out. Don't worry. I'll find someone who has time."

Walt slanted another look at Bryce. "You don't have much time to find someone."

"I know. I'll email our volunteer loop." Panic rising, she knew this was the perfect time to say goodnight. She didn't want to be a source of conflict between father and son. Dakota stood. "Thanks for listening. I need to get home to the fur babies."

Walt glared at his son. "You're really not going to help her?"

"Dad—"

"Enjoy the rest of your evening." She saw her things on a hat tree near the door. "I'll show myself out."

Bryce stood. "I didn't see a car out front. Where did you park?"

"I walked."

"I'll drive you home."

"He's got time to do that," Walt muttered.

She bit back a laugh. "It's not far."

"It's dark," Bryce said.

She looked at Walt, who seemed to be watching the exchange with interest, but he only shrugged. Some help he was.

"This isn't Seattle," she explained. "Marietta is a safe town, and I live only two blocks away."

"A lot can happen in two blocks," Bryce said.

She looked at Walt. "Talk some sense into your son."

"It's cold outside, and you've had a long day. I have to side with Bryce on this one." Walt's words surprised her. "Let my son drive you home. I'll be fine on my own until he gets back."

"I didn't expect this." She looked at both Grayson men. "Two against one, huh?"

Bryce nodded once. So did Walt.

"Looks like this is a battle I'm not going to win." She blew out a breath. "You can drive me home."

Even if doing so is totally unnecessary.

Dakota had to admit his chivalry touched her. She was a tad flattered, too. She'd been sending off a stay-away-from-me vibe for so long, men rarely noticed she was a woman these days. She missed the flirtatious glances, smiles, and compliments. Not enough to start dating again, but being driven home might be a nice change.

Even if Bryce Grayson was the one doing the driving.

Chapter Six

A FEW MINUTES later, Bryce pulled his dad's truck to the curb in front of Dakota's two-story house. The street was well lit and her porchlight was on, but driving her the two blocks was the right thing to do.

The way her lip quivered at his dad's house had made Bryce reach out to her. An instinctive show of support, but leaving his hand on her arm so long had been a conscious move. He'd liked touching her, but he wouldn't do that now.

Even if a part of him wanted to.

The last thing he needed was to find himself forced into helping her with the proposal or something else based on the way his dad kept volunteering him for tasks. What was the big deal about the proposal anyway? She could handle this on her own or find someone else who wanted to help.

He didn't.

Being around Dakota put him on edge. Made him say the wrong things. Had him touching her when he shouldn't.

The best course of action was to avoid her. That

wouldn't be too difficult, even though Marietta was a small town.

He set the parking brake. "Thanks for being a good sport about not walking home."

"Thank you for the ride," Dakota said in a matter-of-fact tone. "I appreciate you and your father's concern over my safety."

"Even if you believe our concern is misplaced."

She unbuckled her seatbelt. "You said it, not me."

Touché.

The style of her house caught his eye. "Your house has a Victorian influence."

"The architect in you is coming out."

"What can I say? A few of my favorite designs have been remodels. I have a soft spot for old houses."

"Me, too, especially for this one." The streetlamp cast shadows on her pretty face. "The house was Victorian, but decades of remodeling by various owners, including my great aunt and uncle, took away or hid those features."

He took a closer look at the home. "It's not that bad."

"Not from the outside, but inside, you can determine the decade a room was remodeled."

"Seriously?"

"It's like living in an *interior design through the twentieth century* exhibit." Dakota half-laughed. "I never noticed when I was a kid, but it's impossible to miss now. We're slowly updating the house and hope to add back some of that

Victorian charm and character."

One of her words stuck out. Bryce had to ask. "We?"

"My great aunt and uncle bought this house in the 1980s, and she left it to me, but my brother and sister help me with remodeling projects when they visit. They both live out of state."

"That's nice of them."

"We have fun." Wistfulness filled Dakota's gaze. "When I was growing up, my two siblings and I would spend a couple of weeks each summer here. Such fond memories."

"Is that why you live in Marietta?"

"Aunt Alice is the main reason I moved here. She needed a housemate, and I needed a place to live."

He wanted to know more. "What's another reason?"

"I was a little kid when I decided to, as my great aunt used to say, 'put down roots' here, but I came to love the town after I moved here as an adult. I guess I'm a small-town girl at heart. When you find the place you belong, you know it." She sounded content. "I wouldn't want to live anywhere else."

The city of Marietta must put something in the water to brainwash people to stay. "I feel the same way about Seattle."

"You just know, right?"

He nodded. Except where he lived was due more to college and finding a job there.

"This house needs a ton of work, but I can visualize the end result," Dakota continued. "My great aunt's been gone for three years, but the remodeling is going slow. Projects happen one at a time and not regularly. Still, I'm making a little progress."

Dakota would make faster progress if she hired his dad. Or maybe his dad was volunteering here, too. Nothing would surprise Bryce at this point. "What have you done so far?"

"Ripped out the carpeting to expose the hardwood floors. Updated some of the older plumbing and wiring. Installed new windows. Removed wallpaper and painted."

"Some of those are expensive updates."

"I hire out the hard stuff or anything that needs a permit."

Interesting. Maybe his dad had been involved with some of the projects.

"But I do what I can myself or with my brother and sister's help," she continued. "My guilty pleasure is watching home improvement shows."

"We have something in common."

"Really?"

He nodded. "I've got to wonder what future generations will think of the subway tile, gray paint, and flooring used in houses today."

"Better than avocado green and harvest gold." She opened the passenger door. "I should let you get back to your father."

"I'll walk you to the door." Bryce didn't want to say

goodnight. Not yet.

"This isn't Seattle."

"I know." He got out of his truck and met her on the sidewalk. "But if Marietta didn't have any crime, there wouldn't be a police department."

She narrowed her gaze. "Is everyone who lives in a big city this paranoid?"

"Not paranoid. Cautious."

Bryce followed her up the steps. The wood creaked beneath his feet. Paint was peeling, but the structure looked solid. He'd love to see the inside, but his father was waiting at home.

The porchlight bathed Dakota in a soft glow. Beautiful.

She looked up at him. "Thanks again for the ride."

"Anytime." And surprisingly, he meant it. "Though I doubt you'll take me up on it again."

Dakota raised her chin. "You never know."

No, you don't.

What Bryce knew was he wanted to kiss her. He didn't know Dakota, but something about her appealed to him in a way he'd never felt. She captivated him.

Maybe it was the way she nurtured those around her. Or maybe it was her sense of humor that kept him off guard at unexpected times. Or maybe it was the easy way she'd forgiven him and accepted his apology.

His gaze traveled from her eyes to her lips.

Soft lips. The kind made for long, hot kisses.

His temperature shot up. His collar tightened.

Bryce wanted to kiss her, but that wasn't why he was here. He straightened. "Keep us posted on what Lori says."

Dakota stuck the key in the knob. "Will do. Thanks again for the ride."

She opened the door.

Something covered in fur bounded out and landed against him. He cringed but, this time, the fight-or-flight response didn't kick in. His muscles, however, tensed into hard knots. He hadn't been prepared for another greeting from the beast. He managed not to be knocked backward, but licking ensued.

More this time.

Bryce cringed. He really didn't like big dogs. A good thing his dad kept hand sanitizer in the glove box.

"Rascal. What are you doing out of the dining room?" Dakota held the dog by the collar. She glanced into the house. "Can you hold him?"

No, but he found himself with the dog anyway.

Dakota ran inside.

Rascal panted and wagged his tail.

Bryce wasn't used to being so close to a big dog or touching one. "You're a friendly beast, right?"

"Oh, no. Pierre. Scout." Panic filled Dakota's voice.

That didn't sound good.

Not wanting to wait for Dakota, Bryce led Rascal into the house, closed the front door, and let the dog lead the way.

A gate lay haphazardly between a wide doorway. Inside the room, a simple light fixture hung from the ceiling. Its location suggested this was a dining room. The walls were painted a pale blue. A large cage lay on its side as if it had fallen off the table. Two black wire dog crates sat nearby. Balls and stuffed animals lay scattered across the scuffed hardwood floor.

Dakota crawled underneath the table. "Thank goodness."

"Is everything okay?" Bryce asked.

"Yes, but for a minute, I thought the worst." She sniffled. "But Pierre and Scout are fine and just taking a nap together the way best buds do."

With one hand on Rascal's collar, Bryce peered around the toppled cage. The small dog was curled up with a gray rat with big ears. Both slept soundly on a pillow.

"That's not something you see every day," he said.

"Not unless you live here." She inched her way from under the table and took Rascal from him.

The dog went willingly. That was good.

Bryce wiped his hand on his pant leg.

She put the dog into one of the crates. "You know better than to make a mess like this."

Rascal deserved the blame. Scout was too small to have jumped onto the table and pushed off the cage. Forget about tearing down the gate.

Bryce kept his distance from the crate. "Rascal's been

busy."

"He has a mind of his own. He's also Scout's minion. Whatever that little dog wants, Rascal does." She surveyed the room. "I rarely leave them out when I'm not around, but they had been crated for so long yesterday, and while I was at work today, that I thought this would be better for them. I never thought I'd be putting Pierre in danger. Or Scout—"

Dakota rubbed her face.

He couldn't see her expression, but her shoulders shook. "It's been a rough twenty-four hours."

Nodding, she wiped her eyes.

Was she…?

That was a tear. Tears.

Not a lot.

But enough.

Bryce wasn't good at this kind of thing. He'd never seen his mom cry until the very end of her life. When former girlfriends had cried, he'd never known what to do or say.

But he got the feeling Dakota needed him to do something now.

Awkwardly, he wrapped his arms around her.

She stiffened. Every muscle tightened beneath his hands.

He should let go. Except… she was leaning into him. Slightly. Maybe he should hold on. He pulled her closer.

She suddenly relaxed and sank against him.

He held onto her tight, not sure what to say, but that seemed to be okay for now.

She drew in a sharp breath. "I-I thought Rascal might have hurt Pierre. Not on purpose, but playing. And that cage could have hit Scout. And…"

He smoothed her hair with his right hand. "It's okay. Everyone is okay."

Holding her like this felt one hundred percent natural. He didn't know why, but he could stand here for the next five minutes or five hours, and be perfectly content. The scent of her vanilla shampoo surrounded him. Her soft breasts pressed against him. Her warmth heated him.

But this wasn't about him. He wanted to comfort her.

"Both Pierre and Scout are fine." Bryce rubbed her back. That seemed to relax her even though she wore a thick coat. "Did you see Rascal? He was relatively calm after his exuberant greeting and licks. He let me bring him into the house and to the dining room."

"Yeah, you didn't freak out this time."

"I didn't freak out the last time." He pulled back slightly and raised her chin with his fingertip. "I never freak out."

No tears fell, but her eyes gleamed. A slight smile returned. "Never?"

Except when dogs were involved or his dad. "On extremely rare occasions."

That brought a smile to Dakota's face.

Bryce let go of her and took a step back.

"Sorry for breaking down," she said. "Like you said, it's been a rough twenty-four hours with little sleep, and I've got so much to do still. I wasn't prepared for anything else to go wrong."

"Especially to animals in your care." He could tell the three might be fosters, but she loved them.

Dakota nodded. "I'm glad you were here even if my eyes must be red and swollen and my face all splotchy."

"Red eyes, yes. Swollen, no. Splotches, not really."

Her smile widened, and then her lips parted.

Bryce wanted to kiss her, but not after what she'd been through. This wasn't the right time. This wasn't…

Dakota kissed him. Just planted her lips against his.

He was shocked but pleased. Very, very pleased.

He followed her lead. Enjoyed the feel of her lips and the way she tasted…

Sweet, warm, and way better than any candy.

She pressed against him. A dog barked.

Rascal.

Dakota jumped back. Eyes wide and cheeks flushed, she touched her mouth and then lowered her hand. "I don't know what I was thinking. I'm sorry. I…I shouldn't have done that."

"I'm happy you did because I wanted to do the same thing."

"You did?"

He nodded. "Just wasn't sure it was the right time."

Uncertainty was written across her face. "Was it?"

Bryce nodded again. "Let's get Rascal's mess cleaned up."

"You don't have to stay."

"Two of us can get this place back together faster." He ran his fingertip along her jawline and fought the urge to kiss her again. "You need sleep more than you need anything else."

Including kisses.

He picked up the cage and set it on the table. Book and papers had been knocked all over the place. He grabbed the papers and straightened them. The first page was marked up as if she'd been proofreading. Lots of crossed out words and scribbles. Some writing he couldn't read.

The books were thick, not pleasure reading. He grabbed them one by one. The first was about living with learning disabilities. Two others were about dyslexia in adults.

Was this why Dakota wanted help on the proposal?

The first one took you a long time to write. Can you have the proposal revised by then and plan an adoption event at the same time?

I'm not worried about the event, but I think… No, I'm going to need help with the report. I just don't know who to ask.

Did his dad know? Was that why he wanted Bryce to help?

But he'd said no.

If he'd known…

Bryce stacked the books before walking to the other side of the table.

He knew now.

She picked up dog toys that had been scattered about the

floor. "Oh, Rascal. You should be the one cleaning up. Not us."

The dog's guilty expression made Bryce smile. Rascal knew he'd done wrong.

"But I still love you, silly boy," she said. "Just please don't do this again."

The love in her voice drew Bryce closer. He kneeled next to her and picked up a ball. "I've been thinking about your proposal. I can help you."

The gratitude in her eyes nearly knocked him over. He placed his hand on the hardwood floor to steady himself.

"Really?" she asked. "That would be great."

Nodding, he wished he'd offered to do this back at his dad's house. "Email me what you have and any notes."

Panic flashed across her face. "Notes?"

That seemed a sore spot. "Or record your ideas using the voice memo app on your phone and send them to me."

Her lips parted as if surprised. "That would work."

Her happy tone pleased him. "I'll leave my contact information."

"Thanks." She picked up a dragon that squeaked. "Did you change your mind about helping because I kissed you?"

"No," Bryce said honestly.

"Good, because I don't plan on doing that again."

He laughed, but he was strangely disappointed. "Glad to know what not to expect."

Her nose scrunched. "So why did you change your

mind?"

Bryce didn't have to think long. He'd made wrong choices over the years—not going home enough to see his mom and dad when they lived in Philadelphia, choosing friends over family when it came time for vacations, and not always being available when people he knew needed help. He wasn't about to do that with Dakota.

He smiled at her. "Because it's the right thing to do."

THURSDAY NIGHT AT Grey's Saloon, Dakota sat with Kelly, her best friend and fellow member of the Chocolate Is Better Than Men Club. The smell of beer hung in the air, but Dakota was drinking ginger ale so she would be clear-headed when she reviewed the revised proposal for the rescue with Bryce later.

She'd kissed him stone-cold sober. Heaven only knew what she'd do if she had a drink. And that was something she didn't want to chance.

"That was nice he helped you clean up," Kelly said.

"Very. I emailed him my proposal last night. We exchanged texts and spoke on the phone before I went to work this morning." Dakota was finishing up telling Kelly what had happened with Bryce. "When I got home after work, an email from him was waiting. There was an attachment. He'd taken my ideas from the voice memos and turned the proposal into a thing of beauty complete with fancy fonts and graphics. Lori won't be able to call it simplistic."

"Great, you sound happy, but let's go back to last night." Kelly's orange-and-navy striped sweater brought out the amber hue in her hazel eyes. Normally, a smile lit up her pretty heart-shaped face, but not tonight. "You really kissed him?"

Of course the kiss was what Kelly would key in on.

Dakota took another sip. A slower one this time. She wasn't ready to answer.

A song about pickup trucks and drinking whiskey played on the jukebox. Two men shot pool. A couple of cowboys chatted up women Dakota didn't recognize.

"Hey. I'm over here." Kelly raised her pint of beer. "Answer me."

"Yes, I kissed him." The words rushed out, a mix of embarrassment and confusion.

"You called him rude and annoying. And let's not forget the fact he lives in Seattle."

All those things were true.

He had apologized and then helped her. So that canceled out him being rude and annoying. But the fact he lived two states away…

Except one kiss didn't mean anything.

Maybe if she kept telling herself that, she'd come to believe it.

Bubbles rose in her glass of ginger ale. Dakota felt as if the same thing was happening in her stomach because of

Bryce. She didn't like the feeling, although she liked the way he'd held her…kissed her back. She moistened her lips.

"You're supposed to be taking a break from dating and men." Kelly leaned over the table. Her hair was haphazardly piled on her head, and a strand fell across her face. She pushed it aside. "Why did you kiss him?"

Dakota wasn't sure how to answer.

His gorgeous eyes and a to-die-for smile had captivated her, but she'd been attracted to those before and never been tempted to kiss him.

His kindness to her at his father's house and driving her home had touched her, but standing on her front porch, she hadn't been tempted to kiss him.

But the way he'd hugged her after her mini-breakdown had rocked her world. He didn't like dogs. At least bigger ones. She could tell by his wariness around Rascal, but he'd somehow understood her fear of something happening to one of the animals—and her being the cause. If her tears had freaked him out, she hadn't known because he'd tried to help, not walk away. There was no way she wasn't going to kiss him.

Dakota raised her glass. Normally, she would tell Kelly everything, but not this time. Those reasons weren't ones to be shared. "Kissing him felt like the right thing to do at the moment."

"Did he mind?"

"Not at all." Dakota laughed. "He said he'd wanted to

kiss me."

Hearing those surprising words had made her want to kiss him again. She'd forgotten how wonderful a kiss could feel. A good thing Rascal had barked so the kiss had been brief or she might have gotten carried away.

Kelly stared over the rim of her pint glass. "Just watch, I'm going to be the only member left in the CIBTM club."

"It was one kiss. And don't forget, he goes back to Seattle at the end of the month."

That red flag told Dakota any more kisses would be a big mistake.

"How did you leave things?" Kelly asked.

"He helped me clean up the dining room, and then he offered to help me with the proposal." Thinking about the time Bryce must have spent making the revisions made Dakota feel special, as if someone was trying to make life easier for her. She hadn't felt that way since before Aunt Alice passed. It made Dakota feel bad for saying Bryce was rude and a jerk, even if he had been.

Kelly laughed. "If that goofy smile on your face is any indication, I'd say you have yourself a man crush."

"It's called gratitude."

She took a drink. "If you say so, but I think you have a heavy case of denial going on."

Dakota wiped a bead of condensation off her glass. "I don't."

At least, she didn't think she did.

"You're afraid of getting hurt again," Kelly said. "That makes total sense after what you went through with Craig, but you seem to like Bryce, and though he's had his moments, he might not be another Mr. Wrong."

"He lives in Seattle, so he isn't Mr. Right."

"A man doesn't have to be one or the other. He can fall in between. A Mr. Maybe or a Mr. Right Now. You'd need to keep things casual since you know there's an end date."

Casual still sounded scary. Knowing when things would end gave Dakota a chill. She bit her lip. Starting something that had no chance of going anywhere sounded like a bad idea. "I don't know."

"I do." Kelly sounded certain. "You're obviously fangirling over the guy, so why not go for it?"

Dakota slumped in her chair. "You're supposed to be on my side and talk me out of wanting to go out with Bryce. Men."

Kelly grinned, a wide smile that brightened her face and drew the attention of a cowboy sitting alone at the bar. "If I thought you didn't like him or that he might not be good for you, I would."

Cheers erupted from the pool table.

"Having a built-in end date is a good thing. It'll keep things from getting too serious. Having fun while he's in town would be good for you."

"I've never dated casually."

"You need to do this." Kelly rubbed her chin. "Bryce

might be exactly what you need to get your dating mojo back."

Dakota blew out a breath. "I've never had any mojo."

"Then it's time to get some." The excitement in Kelly's eyes matched her voice. "Go out with him. See what happens."

"You're talking like he wants to go out with me. Offering to help with my proposal isn't a romantic gesture."

"No, but it's a start. And if he did ask you out…"

The question floated on the air like a cloud of smoke. Bryce was far from perfect, but he cared about his father enough to spend a month in Marietta and help out at the rescue because the place was important to Walt. Bryce hadn't left her to clean up Rascal's mess on her own, and he'd rewritten her proposal.

Were those enough signs to tell her he wasn't another Mr. Wrong? She hoped so, but doubts swirled through her head. The list of what could go wrong was twice as long as what could go right.

"I'm not sure I'm ready to go out with anyone. I know I'm being safe and cautious, but that's the way my heart wants me to be."

"Your heart is going to get lonely."

The kiss had made her feel good, content even, but did she need more than that right now? "Better lonely than broken."

Kelly reached across the table and touched Dakota's

hand. "I know this is going to be hard for you, but I want you to think about it. Please."

"I will."

"I also want you to promise me one thing."

The hair on the back of her neck stood up. "What?"

"If Bryce asks you out, promise me you won't be so quick to stay no. Consider what you have to lose by going on *one* date. It might not be as much as you think."

Or it could be way more than Dakota was willing to risk.

But what were the odds she'd have to make that choice?

Slim to none, she'd guess.

That bummed her out.

A part of her wanted to be asked her out, even though she knew wishes—especially hers—didn't always match up with reality. Still, she would do this for herself and for Kelly.

Under the table, she crossed the fingers on her left hand. She raised her glass in her right hand as if making a toast. "Okay, I promise."

Chapter Seven

LATER THAT NIGHT, Bryce sat in the kitchen with Dakota across the table from him. His dad had gone to bed an hour ago. Which was a good thing because they had a lot of work to do.

Bryce's laptop was open with the revised proposal on the screen. Print copies of the pages lay between them. Some had been proofed. Others still needed to be.

He should be focused on the changes they'd been making for the past forty minutes, but he was more interested in Dakota.

As she looked over one of the pages, her face was a portrait in concentration. Her gaze narrowed, and her lips moved as she silently read to herself.

He'd been thinking about the way she'd kissed him the other night. If Rascal hadn't barked, would she have kept kissing him? He liked to think so because he wouldn't have stopped. His curiosity about her plans to go out after work tonight—ones she hadn't wanted to change—was also growing. "We're making good progress."

"Thanks for meeting so late."

"No problem." He twirled his pen with his fingers. "Did you have fun earlier?"

She nodded.

Bryce picked up a piece of paper but didn't read any of the words. "Where did you go?"

"Grey's Saloon."

His dad had mentioned the bar on Main Street. "Was it crowded?"

"No, not for a Thursday night. A few new faces, but mostly regulars were there."

Was she a regular? Not that it mattered, but he wanted to know. She didn't act like she'd been drinking or seem the type to pick up guys in bars. Maybe there was a side to her he hadn't seen. "Is that where you hang out?"

"Sometimes."

"I heard it's the happening place in town."

"Somedays. You should go."

It didn't sound like he'd be going with her. Surprisingly, that bothered him, though he wasn't sure why. He enjoyed spending time with Dakota, but he wasn't looking for a date. "I'll check it out before I leave."

She gave him the once over. "Do, but you might feel more comfortable at the Graff Hotel. That place draws a more dressed-up crowd."

He glanced down at his button-down shirt, sweater, and khakis. "I'm not dressed up."

Amusement filled her gaze. "For Marietta you are."

Bryce wondered if that comment meant she preferred cowboys. Men in faded jeans and boots.

She reached across the table with a piece of paper in her hand. "What do you think about the changes to the foster program fundraising section?"

Dakota was changing the subject. Still, Bryce read the section.

"Much clearer. Good job, except…" He crossed out a word and wrote a different one. "This word should be capital, not capitol. I mix them up all the time myself, and it's something spellcheck won't mark."

"I don't know what I'd do without spellcheck." She flushed. "I struggle a bit with the written word."

"When was the last time you wrote anything like this?"

"College." She folded the corner of one of the pages. "Not a big fan of term papers or reading. I prefer audio books."

"Those are great for the car or gym."

Nodding, she opened her mouth and then closed it.

"The only reading I have time for these days is on my cell phone."

She looked down at a piece of paper before looking back at him.

Something was going on. "Anything wrong?"

"There's a reason I needed your help with the proposal. I, um, found out my freshman year that I had…have…a learning disability." The way she averted her gaze from his told Bryce saying these words wasn't easy for her. "Knowing why I had trouble helped, but I still get frustrated at times. Not a lot of people know, and I...I really appreciate your help with this today."

He hadn't expected her to tell him. His respect grew, and he felt...honored that she'd trusted him with the information. "The original version of your proposal was good."

"Lori called it simplistic."

Bryce heard the hurt in the words. He touched the top of Dakota's hand. "No, it was short and to the point. Nothing wrong with that. Except...when you're asking for money to fund a project, the less-is-more approach doesn't always work."

"I'll have to remember that." Her features relaxed.

"Plan on doing more of these?"

She shrugged. "I do what I'm asked."

"Even if it's hard?"

She nodded. "But finding animals homes is important."

"I'm happy you're pleased with the revised proposal."

"Thrilled," she admitted, and her sincere tone made him sit taller. "I hope you know your help with the *Home for Thanksgiving* program will make a big difference to the animals at Whiskers and Paw Pals."

"Thanks, but don't tell my dad. I fear he's already trying to convert me into an animal rescuer."

"I won't." She laughed. "My great aunt took pride in

indoctrinating me. That was the word she used, too. Her dream was to start an animal rescue. I wanted that, too, but she was getting too old, and I didn't feel I had the skills on my own."

Bryce pointed to the pages they'd been reviewing. "You have the knowledge. Based on what my dad says, the skills, too."

She shrugged. "Skills might be the wrong word. More like confidence."

"That will come." Bryce realized he was still touching her. He drew back his hand. "Maybe you just need a little push in that direction."

"I don't know about that. As long as Lori keeps Whiskers and Paw Pals going, there isn't a need for yet another rescue in town."

"That sounds like an excuse."

"A practical one, maybe." She grinned and then picked up another page. "We'd better get busy or we'll be here all night."

She was right, but that didn't sound like a bad option to him.

Until he remembered his dad.

Bryce wasn't here to date a pretty woman from a small town. He was here to help his father recover and convince him to move to Seattle. If that included helping the animal rescue and Dakota, so be it. But that was where his involvement with the woman across the table and the animals she loved needed to end.

He had to stay focused on the end goal.

Prying Walt Grayson away from Marietta wasn't going to be easy. Dad didn't want to discuss moving at all. Too bad. It was going to happen after Thanksgiving.

Bryce would find a way. No matter what it took.

THE ALARM RANG, and, for once, Dakota didn't hit snooze. She didn't need the extra sleep this morning.

A first.

By the time she'd gotten home from Walt's and taken care of the animals last night, she'd been yawning as she walked up the stairs. A quick change into jammies, and she'd had no difficulty falling asleep. No tossing and turning, unable to get comfortable. No waking up in the middle of the night with a million thoughts on her mind.

Not normal for her.

But she hoped this was the first of many nights like that.

She crawled out of bed.

With the rescue closed, she would swing by Lori's place and then drive to Bozeman. She needed to visit Maverick, the sweet Border collie, and buy what she needed for this weekend's adoption event. She'd be back in time to set up the area inside the feed store.

Her cell phone beeped.

She grabbed it from the nightstand.

Kelly: *How did last night go?*

Dakota: *Great. The revised proposal is even better now.*

Kelly: *I meant with Bryce.*

Dakota: *We worked.*

Kelly: *Nothing else?*

Dakota: *Nope.*

Kelly: *Bummer.*

Dakota: *I told you he's not interested.*

Kelly: *His loss.*

Kelly: *BTW, that cowboy alone at the bar asked me out after you left. I said yes.*

Dakota: *Happy you're taking your own advice.*

Kelly: *Knew you would say that.*

Kelly: *TTYL. Zumba class to teach.*

His loss. Kelly was too much, but that was what friends were for. Dakota hoped her best friend had fun with that cowboy.

Dakota had enjoyed working with Bryce yesterday. He didn't make her feel like she took too much time or made too many mistakes. She hadn't planned to tell him about her learning disability, but the words had just come out.

She hoped she didn't regret that.

But then again, he was leaving after Thanksgiving. And she hoped people wouldn't care if they found out about her reading issue.

Her phone beeped again.

Bryce: *Is it ready to go?*

Dakota: *Yes! Dropping off this morning.*

Dakota: *Thanks again.*

Bryce: *Anytime. Have a good day.*

She only wished he meant that. Not about her day. She tried to make each one good, but about his helping her anytime.

She'd liked sitting with him at the kitchen table. The back and forth. The splitting tasks. The way he touched her hand.

Was her heart already lonely? Kelly seemed to think Dakota was headed in that direction.

She didn't know, but last night, she'd felt a sense of teamwork and contentment with Bryce. She hadn't felt that way with any guy she'd dated, including Craig.

Maybe she was closer to wanting to date again?

But that part of her had been shut off for so long, would a man want to go out with her?

She stared at her reflection in the mirror above her dresser. Her hair was a tangled mess, and her face paler than normal.

Would Bryce?

The thought made her heart beat too fast. She turned away from the mirror. *Not going there. Casual, remember?* The heart wasn't allowed to be involved at all.

FRIDAY AFTER LUNCH, Bryce sat in the waiting room of his father's physician. Nothing serious, a routine follow-up visit for his dad, but the lighting and smells reminded Bryce of his mom's time in the hospital and her final day at home on hospice.

She'd talked about taking a vacation that upcoming Thanksgiving. They could meet in the middle of the US, Chicago maybe. She'd also wanted him to come home for Christmas, too. Something he hadn't done in years. She'd offered to have her and Dad fly to Seattle if that would be easier. But her dream of the three of them finally spending a holiday together had died with her.

Bryce crossed and the uncrossed his legs. That didn't help him feel more comfortable.

He rose and poured himself a cup of coffee. That might quench his thirst and stop the ache in his throat.

He took a sip of the hot liquid. Better.

Sitting down on the same chair, he stared at the pile of magazines on his left. Not one had kept his attention. He didn't care what couple was breaking up or if two movie stars wore the same dress to an event.

He pulled out his cell phone, scanned his inbox, read an email from the contractor who'd been picked to repair the water damage at the rescue, and texted with his assistant in Seattle.

He'd worked on Dakota's proposal yesterday, not his own. He needed to make sure he didn't fall behind his schedule. If he were awarded this contract, his design firm would rise in the ranks.

Bryce wanted that. Badly.

A ballad played from hidden speakers. The lyrics spoke about slow kisses, dancing beneath the moonlight, and love lost and found.

The song reminded him of Dakota.

Stop.

Her revised proposal had been turned in. She no longer needed his help. He had to stopping thinking about her.

Nothing could interfere with his plans for his dad. Not even a caring woman who put everyone else first whether they had two legs or four, made him laugh, and kissed like a dream.

A nurse pushed his father in the wheelchair. "He's ready to go."

"Told you it wouldn't take long." His father was talking to Bryce, but he was smiling at the pretty nurse with dark hair and brown eyes. "Doc Gallagher says I'm doing well."

"You'll have to start doing more around the house then."

His dad shook his head. "Exactly as I've been saying."

Less than ten minutes later, he had his dad situated in the wheelchair accessible van they'd rented. "Let's get you home."

"The sooner, the better," his father said from the backseat. "I've got friends coming over to visit."

"You've turned into Mr. Social. You always have friends

stopping by. Or your construction crew."

"Ted likes to keep me updated on the jobs."

"And eat chocolate."

"That too."

"You were never like this in Philadelphia."

"Your mom would have liked to have more of a community." His dad sounded wistful. "But I worked too much."

"She could have done it herself."

"Not without a push from me, and once I got home, I didn't want to go out or have to deal with other people."

Bryce didn't remember his dad being that way. He always showed up at games and school functions. Maybe he meant social events. "And now?"

"It's not as bad as I thought it would be."

"You could do the same in Seattle."

His father covered his ears like a kid. "I'm not listening."

Bryce tightened his grip on the steering wheel. He'd bring this up again later.

"After my friends arrive, I need you to run to the feed store."

That was odd. "Why the feed store? You don't have animals."

"They sell more than food. I want you to buy a pair of heavy-duty work socks."

What was going on? Bryce glanced in the rearview mirror. "Did Dr. Gallagher give you pain meds?"

"Nope. Don't need them. Chocolate is the best medicine."

Maybe there wasn't something in the town water supply, but in the chocolate. "Uh, Dad… you have casts on both your legs. You can't wear socks."

Dad grinned. "The socks are for you. Ted thought you might want to tour the job sites and report back. You'll need more than your city-slicker dress socks you wear with those fancy I-talian leather shoes."

His father made him sound like a fashionista. Bryce wasn't. He dressed like everyone else he knew. But he had packed work items just in case. "I brought other socks. For my boots."

"Trust me, you need new ones," his father urged. "Humor an old man."

Now that was funny given past conversations. "Old man?"

"Figure of speech to elicit sympathy. Did it work?"

He loved his dad, but, as his mother used to say, the man sure knew how to push his buttons. "I haven't decided."

Another glance in the mirror showed the hard set of his father's jaw—a telltale sign of his stubbornness about to set in. If that happened, the rest of the day would go downhill fast.

"Make up your mind," his dad said.

"I'll buy a pair of socks."

A smug smiled settled on his dad's face. "Excellent decision. I'll pay for them."

"I've got my own money."

"Suit yourself. And there's no need for you to rush back home."

His dad was acting strange. Maybe he had an ulterior motive for wanting him to go to the shop. "Are you trying to get rid of me? Are friends coming over or a special one?"

"Friends. Plural. I just hate to see you stuck at home all the time."

This place wasn't Bryce's home. "I'm here to help you."

"Then help me by going to the feed store."

At least his father hadn't wanted Bryce to go back to the chocolate shop. He didn't want to seem like a stalker or for Dakota to think he was interested in her.

Yes, he was attracted, but that was as far as he could let it go.

INSIDE THE FEED store, Dakota checked on Rascal and Scout in their portable crates. The two dogs stared at her with love and trust. The same way they'd done when she'd put them in hard sided crates to drive to Bozeman and when she'd arrived here.

"This won't take me too long to set up," she said to them. "Once I finish, we'll go for a long walk."

Rascal's mouth hung open in what she called his smile.

Scout walked in a small circle, as if trying to catch his tail, until he lay in the crate all curled up and comfy.

She studied the area that Tim, the feed store's owner, had cleared for the event. People could shop and see the animal at the same time. A win-win. And much better than having an event outside this time of year. Tim had adopted a dog from Whiskers and Paw Pals and had become a big rescue supporter after that. This wasn't the first event they'd held here, but this two-day adoption drive would have more animals than usual since so many were being temporarily housed elsewhere.

"Better get started."

Rascal's tail wagged faster.

"You've been so good today, but you should rest up for your walk like Scout."

The dog remained on all fours.

"Okay, watch if you like, but you'll be tired later."

She setup the first folding table. "Brochures and info sheets can go here."

Rascal continued to watch her. Scout's eyes had closed. The excitement of visiting Janie O'Brien's rescue in Bozeman had worn out the little dog.

Would these two get adopted tomorrow?

A steel clamp gripped Dakota's heart and squeezed.

If that happened, it would just be her and Pierre.

She forced herself to breathe.

No problem. She'd been through this before. More times than she could count. Adoptions were a bittersweet moment, but she knew to be happier for the dog and their family than sad for herself.

"I hope you and everyone else finds a home tomorrow," she said to Rascal. "Then we wouldn't have to worry about what the benefactor says about our requests."

That was Lori's word. *Requests.* Dakota preferred *demands.* She also wondered who the benefactor might be, but since that person was going through an attorney, they might never find out.

Rascal barked.

She looked at the dog. "You agree with me."

"Of course he does."

Dakota spun. "Bryce?"

He wore navy slacks, a blue-and-green striped shirt, and a forest green quilted coat. Her pulse kicked up a notch.

He had city slicker written all over his clean-shaven face, but the style fit him, even though she'd love to see him wearing a pair of faded jeans, a button-down western shirt, scuffed boots, and a cowboy hat. Though, she had to admit, either way he looked nice. Okay, yummy.

"If anyone can pull this off, it's you."

His words gave her a confidence boost. She pushed her shoulders back. "Thanks."

Bryce walked toward her with the ease of an athlete. He must run or work out.

Maybe she'd been too quick to discount city guys. He wasn't one of those sit-behind-a-desk types. He worked with his hands and wasn't afraid to get dirty. Other than his clothes, he could hold his own against a few cowboys. Still, he would look hot in a hat.

His intense gaze made her feel like the only remaining box of truffles in the shop on Valentine's Day.

Her heart rate accelerated and caught up to her speeding pulse. She cleared her dry throat. "What are you doing here?"

"My father's playing bridge with three friends, and he sent me here to buy a pair of socks."

That wasn't the answer she'd been expecting. "Socks?"

"I see now it was an excuse."

"To get you out of the house so he could play cards?"

"To get me here."

Tim sold clothing, gardening items, and other things besides animal feed and pet supplies, but a store like this was last place a guy like Bryce would shop. "Why?"

A wry grin formed. "Because you're here."

"Me?"

"It appears matchmaking, not cards, is my father's new hobby."

"Oh, no." Her cheeks burned. "I guess that explains why he's been pushing you to help with the animal rescue."

"And buying chocolate every day."

"Before your dad broke his legs, he stopped by the shop almost every day."

"He didn't ask me to go today. It's your day off, right?"

Oh, Walt. She rubbed her neck. He was one of her closest friends, but what was he thinking? "Yes. I only work

Tuesdays, Wednesdays, and Thursdays."

"Those are the days he's sent me to the chocolate shop. He's matchmaking."

Bryce's grin reached his eyes and made her legs wobble. She steadied herself against the table. No man had the right to be that good looking. And why wasn't he upset at his father's antics? If anything, Bryce appeared amused, not angry.

"I'm sorry," she said.

"Not your fault. This is all on my dad." Bryce came closer.

She caught a whiff of him. Not aftershave, but soap again—masculine with a touch of spice, maybe mint. She liked the way he smelled. A little too much.

Dakota took a step back. "You'd better buy those socks so he doesn't know you're onto him."

"I will, but, at some point, I'm going to tell him he's been busted."

She couldn't tell if Bryce thought this was funny or not. She imagined he'd be more than a little annoyed at his father. "Your dad only has your best interests at heart."

"And yours." Bryce half-laughed. "For all I know, he and his card-playing cronies are all in this together."

The thought made her cringe. "I sure hope not."

"Don't worry. I'll make sure this stops."

"Be nice about it."

"I'm always nice."

"Not always." At least, he hadn't been with her at first. "But you apologized for that."

"You're right. I'll make a conscious effort with my dad. Okay?"

She nodded.

Bryce looked around. "What are you doing?"

"Setting up for this weekend's adoption drive."

"You said you had volunteers to help."

"This is a last-minute event. People will be here Saturday and Sunday, but today was too short of notice."

He slipped off his jacket. "I'll help."

Bryce had helped the night of the water damage and with the revised proposal because of his dad. Walt might have sent Bryce here this afternoon, but he was offering to help on his own. She appreciated that. It endeared him to her all the more, but she wasn't sure what to say.

"You'll ruin your nice clothes moving stuff around."

"I'll take my chances." He placed his hands on his hips and puffed out his chest like a superhero. "Besides, moving stuff around is one of my specialties."

Dakota didn't want to be charmed, but a smile tugged on the corners of her mouth. The smartest move would be to tell Bryce that she had this under control, which she did. Still, a part of her wanted him to stay. She could use an extra set of hands. She also liked spending time with him. "Are you sure?"

Rascal barked as if answering for Bryce.

"Positive," he said.

"O-kay." She blew out a breath and pointed to where she envisioned things going. Thank goodness Tim allowed them to set-up today or tomorrow they'd have to arrive before sunrise. "We need to set up a row of tables and then cover them with the Thanksgiving-themed tablecloths I bought in Bozeman at the dollar store this morning."

He grabbed one of the tables, unfolded it, and fastened the legs. "You get around."

"Some days more than others."

She'd not only gone to shop, but also to visit Maverick, as she'd promised him, and ask—okay, beg—for Janie O'Brien's help finding adopters. Of course, her aunt's longtime animal rescue friend, and now Dakota's friend, had agreed.

She motioned to the dogs. "Today, I had company. They like car rides."

Bryce glanced at the crates. "Where's Pierre?"

"He's not a fan of car rides." She lifted a table. Bryce took it out of her hands. She gave him a look. "I'm the one who usually does this. Sometimes on my own."

"I know, but since I'm here, how about I set up the tables and you cover them?"

Arguing would only waste time. The dogs would want out of the crates soon. Well, Rascal. Scout was asleep. "I can do that."

She unwrapped the plastic from the table coverings.

Bryce lifted a table as if it weighed nothing. She struggled when doing the setup on her own. One by one, he unfolded and put them into place.

She carried over the table coverings. "You're fast."

"With things like this, yes. With other things, I like to take my time."

Her temperature spiked. She wanted to know what other things, and if the playful and sexy images forming in her mind were what he meant. She clamped down her thoughts and focused on the task at hand.

She covered the first table.

"The tables are set up. I'll help you." He reached for one of the tablecloths, and his hand brushed hers.

No spark, but heat pulsed at the point of contact.

She took a step back and bumped into him.

His hands went around her waist to steady her. Large, warm hands. Ones that felt good on her.

What was she thinking? He was trying to help her, not make a move. Heat rushed up her neck.

He let go of her, and she wished he hadn't. She liked him touching her. And that was a problem.

"Sorry." The word shot out of her mouth. She needed to say something. "I didn't see you."

"You couldn't see me. I was right behind you."

"I'll be more careful."

A lot more careful when he was around.

"Me, too."

She went back to covering the tables, and so did he.

Less than an hour later, they were ready for the animals and volunteers to arrive in the morning.

"That was fast." With a mixture of relief and surprise, Dakota stared at the tables and the open space where the dogs would meet and greet potential adopters. "This usually takes me at least two hours to do on my own."

A satisfied grin formed on Bryce's face. "We work well together."

She'd been thinking the same thing. "Don't tell your dad."

Bryce laughed. "I won't."

"Four hands work faster than two." Dakota wanted to do something to show her gratitude, but a hug seemed too personal and she needed to avoid more kisses. Though that was exactly what she wanted. She settled for words of gratitude. "Thank you. Your help meant a lot to me."

"What's next?" he asked.

She held up her hands. "Your work is done. Buy your socks and go home."

"I'd rather stay with you."

A warm and fuzzy feeling flowed through her. That should bother her more than it did. She eyed him. "Don't you want to check on your dad?"

"Bridge takes forever to play. I have time before I need to go back."

She felt torn between what she wanted to do and what

she should do. She loved her foster rat and dogs, and she wasn't that lonely. But would chocolate and animals be enough in the future?

Maybe Kelly was right about Bryce being the guy to get her back in the dating game. If he was as nice a guy as he seemed, then maybe Dakota wasn't doomed to pick Mr. Wrongs.

Face it, she wasn't ready for anything serious, so his living in Seattle was actually good. Nothing long term was possible with a guy who lived so far away. She could dip her toe into the dating pool and just have fun.

Some mojo would be good, right?

Dakota took a breath. And another. "I'm going to put the portable crates in the car and take Scout and Rascal on a walk. Do you want to come with us?"

He looked at the dogs.

The hesitation and uncertainty in his eyes made her stomach drop. He was going to say no.

"It's been a long time since I've walked a dog. The beast might be too much for me. Could I hold Scout's leash?"

He wanted to go! Warmth flowed through her. "Of course. Rascal can be a handful."

Dakota bit back a laugh. She only hoped she could handle Bryce better than that puppy.

Chapter Eight

WALKING DOGS WITH Dakota on a crisp autumn Friday afternoon wasn't so bad. Bryce held onto Scout's leash and shortened his stride. The small dog reminded him of his childhood pet Spartacus. Non-threatening and one hundred percent loveable. The little guy didn't bark. He just pumped his shorter legs to keep up with everyone else.

Rascal, however, was another story.

Dakota held onto his leash and walked between Bryce and the dog. She worked to control Rascal, who seemed to want to go in every direction except forward, but not once did she lose her patience. Her voice was strong and firm, but never too loud. The more Bryce learned about Dakota Parker, the more impressed he was.

Rascal wasn't a beast, but his size reminded Bryce of that dog who had chased him years ago. He was older and bigger now. Logically, he knew this wasn't the same animal and he had no reason to worry, but he kept his distance from the clumsy, energetic puppy anyway. Caution seemed the prudent course here.

"The dogs like to walk," he said.

"Yes. All I have to do is touch their leashes and they start jumping like pogo sticks." The look of adoration she showered on the two dogs made Bryce wish she'd look at him like that. "It's so cute."

She was cute. Beautiful, really. Even though clouds were moving in, the daylight brought out the blonde highlights in her hair. Her brown eyes were warm and reminded him of the delicious chocolate she sold. And her easy smile was contagious to both man and beast. Well, beasts if Rascal counted.

"Do you usually walk them on your own?" Bryce asked.

"Yes. I shoot for twice a day, but if not, I have a dog run in the backyard. Scout's not a big fan of that. He much prefers running in the hallways indoors, but Rascal loves it."

Bryce laughed. "Is there anything Rascal doesn't love?"

"Obeying." She shortened the leash to keep him away from a child's bicycle in a front yard.

"He seems curious."

"That's a puppy for you."

A dirty, dented pickup truck drove past. A man in a cowboy hat sat behind the wheel and honked the horn. He lifted his hat.

Dakota waved.

"Friend of yours?" Bryce asked.

"A wrangler from a ranch outside of town."

That didn't tell him if the cowboy was a friend...or more. "You must know everyone around here."

"If they're regulars at the chocolate shop, I do. But some I know through Whiskers and Paw Pals, others from my summer vacations here as a kid, and a few from various places in town. You'll find a nice cross-section of people in Marietta and the surrounding areas."

"You've studied this?"

"Anecdotally, but I majored in Sociology with the thought of possibly going to law school, but I decided that wasn't for me. My father was in the army, so we saw many parts of the world. I learned how to get a feel for a place and the people there quickly."

"The world at your disposal and here you are."

"Marietta makes me happy."

"Don't you get bored?"

"You can be bored anywhere, not just living in the country." She stopped to let Rascal sniff a tree. Scout followed him. "I don't have much free time between my job at the chocolate shop and volunteering at the animal rescue, but there's enough for me to do. Don't forget, Bozeman and Livingston aren't far if I need a change of scenery."

Bryce hadn't been to those towns. He'd been sticking close to his father's house other than errands or appointments. "There's not a big population."

"No, and those who live here know everybody's business."

Whatever attracted the dogs to the tree no longer seemed interesting to them. Rascal lumbered away. Scout pranced like a show pony. Not the manliest of dogs, but those tiny legs of his could move.

He'd overheard some conversations during his father's card games. "Doesn't that nosiness bother you?"

Dakota shrugged. "That nosiness is part of small-town living. It can be hard when you're single and dating or you break up, but I'd rather have people knowing too much than live in a big city where no one cares what's going on."

"People care where I live." He'd received calls after his dad's fall. A friend was watching his condo. His assistant was taking care of the mail, bills, and business. "But life is busier there."

"Life is busy everywhere, but I've had an easier time forming relationships in Marietta."

Friendships or romantic relationships? Bryce rubbed the back of this neck. He shouldn't care, yet he wanted to know. "Many of my friends stayed in Seattle after we graduated from UW."

"Having a built-in community must have been nice as you transitioned from school to working."

He nodded. "Instead of going to classes, we went to jobs, but not much else changed other than us having more money. We went to happy hours during the week and watched sports on the weekends."

"And now?"

Bryce had to think about that for a moment. "We don't see each other as much. People have careers and families, often a combo of the two."

That made him wonder how often his dad had gotten together with friends before his accident. Bryce couldn't imagine it was as much as now, but maybe older people had more time on their hands. Although, his dad had worked full time and volunteered before breaking his legs.

The sun dipped lower in the sky, but the temperature hadn't dropped. Or maybe he was warm from the walk.

Scout barked, a high-pitched squeal that sounded more like a battery-operated toy than a real dog.

Bryce scooped up the ball of fur. "Need a rest, little guy?"

Scout panted. His pink tongue hung out of his mouth.

Bryce couldn't tell what the dog wanted or why, but the pooch weighed less than a bag of flour.

Dakota quickened her pace. "Scout has you trained already."

"His short legs have to walk farther and faster than ours, so he gets tired."

"Did Scout tell you that?" she teased.

"Not in so many words, but he wants to rest."

Bryce scratched behind Scout's ear. The dog soaked up the attention.

Dakota stared at him. "Looks like you're correct."

"Of course I am." Bet Scout was one of the lap-dog

types. That was Bryce's kind of dog. "Do you think Scout will be adopted this weekend?"

"There's no reason he shouldn't be. It's a matter of the right adopter seeing him. The only reason I've been keeping him at the house is Pierre. I hope we can find them a quiet home together."

Bryce remembered the two sleeping on the pillow the other night. "Did they come as a pair?"

"No, but they bonded at my house. Pierre first nested in Scout's hair. The rat now grooms him, too."

"I hope they can stay together."

"Me, too, but sometimes that's not an option. Placing a bonded pair can be more difficult."

Bryce held Scout closer and hoped the dog and the rat found someone who wanted both of them. "Is it hard when one of your foster animals is adopted?"

"You get attached. At least, I do. But it's hard to stay sad when an animal you care about is adopted by a loving family." Those gold flecks in her brown eyes glowed like flames. She gave Rascal a pat on the side of the neck. "That's why I do this. To find each of them a forever home."

The emotion in her voice told him she loved what she did. She was lucky to have found that. Some never did.

"Have you considered adopting your own pet instead of fostering?" he asked.

"Not seriously."

Her words surprised him. "Why not?"

"I can do more as a foster. Especially for those animals like Rascal who need training and socializing before being placed."

"You're a dog whisperer."

She laughed. "I rarely whisper. Especially with this big guy who can't seem to hear me. Though he's doing better."

"He didn't go crazy when he saw me."

"That's because he was in the crate, but he was happy to see you."

Had Dakota been happy to see him?

She seemed more surprised, but she'd smiled. That had to be a good sign.

"Have you been tempted to keep a foster animal?" Bryce asked.

"Whiskers and Paw Pals has had many foster failures— that's what it's called when a foster ends up adopting their foster animal. It's not really a failure since a good match was made, and I'm hoping some of our emergency fosters decide to adopt who they have in their care, but that's never happened to me. I've thought about keeping a couple of animals in the past. We moved so much when I was younger we didn't have any pets, but whenever I'm tempted to make things permanent, I realize the animals are better off with a family, someone who works from home, or a million other things."

"You're selling yourself short."

"I want to do what's best for the animal, and that means

leaving myself out of the equation."

"You make it sound so logical."

"Oh, there's plenty of emotion involved. I've cried like crazy after placing animals because I was going to miss them."

"That must be hard."

She shrugged. "Animal rescue can be exhausting, frustrating, and heartbreaking, but when you find an animal the right home, you forget all that."

"Have you thought about stopping?"

She half-laughed. "I tried once. Took a break. But within days, a pregnant cat made herself at home on my porch. Next thing I knew, five newborn kittens were out there."

"So even when you're not looking to help animals—"

"They find me," she finished for him. "Must be some underground animal network out there. They know where we live."

She sounded amused by that. "You don't mind."

"Nope. The love you get in return is worth everything you go through, even if you only have an animal a short time."

"Even if you lose them?"

Her gaze clouded but cleared again an instant later. "Even then."

Scout's eyes were closed. He'd fallen asleep.

"We had a pug named Spartacus when I was younger. He used to sleep with me. After he died, my parents didn't want another pet."

"People often make that choice."

"I thought it was the wrong decision back then, but I was a teenager, so what did I know? All I did was play fetch with Spartacus and occasionally scoop poop from the backyard. My parents, really my mom, did all the work."

"Have you ever considered adopting a pet?"

"No," he answered quickly. "I live in a condo, and I'm away too much."

"Where do you go?" she asked.

"My office, job sites, out."

He waited for her to launch into a spiel about why he should adopt.

"I'm fortunate I can run home from the chocolate shop to spend time with the dogs during my breaks," she said instead. "I'm allowed to take them with me to the rescue."

"Must be nice."

She stared at Rascal. "No complaints."

Bryce kept waiting for her to launch into her sales pitch for adoption. After she didn't, he asked, "Aren't you going to try to talk me into adopting?"

"Adopting an animal is a commitment and decision that must be made by the adopter, no one else. Not everyone is ready or able to care for an animal."

The gold flecks in her eyes glowed bright. So beautiful.

"You are so passionate about animals," he said.

"Animals and chocolate."

Bryce laughed, but did her words mean she wasn't dating? He hoped that was the case. Not that her dating status would change anything.

He was only in Marietta for the month. A month to care for his dad and convince him Seattle was the right move.

Bryce wasn't looking for a relationship, but he wanted to get to know Dakota better. Something about her appealed to him at a gut level. In a way that few, if any, women had in the past. He wished he could explain the feeling, but it was just there and kept growing.

She worked so hard and cared so deeply. He was tempted to see if he could make the gold flecks in her eyes light up again. Would they glow like embers or sparkle like fireworks?

No matter how much he tried to put her kiss behind him, he hadn't. Only this time, he wanted to kiss her.

But for some reason, he had the feeling he wouldn't get the chance.

WALKING DOGS WITH a guy shouldn't be so fun. It never had been in the past, but with Bryce, Dakota couldn't imagine anything better. Poop bags put a damper on the romance, but she enjoyed talking and being with him. He was different from the men who lived around here, and his life in Seattle intrigued her.

Up ahead, she saw Walt's house. The truck was parked in the driveway. The van was still at the feed store. "Do you want to stop by and see how your dad is doing?"

"Sure." Bryce pointed at Rascal. "The big guy might want water."

His concern over the puppy touched her. The way he cradled a sleeping Scout like a baby appealed to her as an animal lover and a woman. City guy or not, Bryce Grayson was downright sexy. He seemed too good to be true.

Was he?

Probably.

Being with him felt like white water rafting on the Gallatin River with her stomach dropping and then lodging in her throat. She was enjoying the ride. Their conversation invigorated her. Concerns over the adoption event faded away with each step they took.

Dakota wanted to open herself up, not close herself off. A weird feeling given this past year.

She must finally be ready to start dating again. That was a good thing, right?

"It's close to dinnertime," Bryce said. "Are you hungry?"

Lunch had been an order of fries and a milkshake on the drive back from Bozeman. "I could eat something."

"Have dinner with us."

Us. Bryce and his dad.

Not a date. She shouldn't feel a stab of disappointment. "I'd like that, but check with your dad. I don't want to intrude if he has other plans."

Bryce smiled. "The man has two broken legs. There are

no other plans."

He had a point, but she didn't want to just burst in on their family dinner. "If you're sure he won't mind…"

"He won't. Trust me."

Could she trust him? She wanted to.

Bryce stared at the dog in his arms. "Scout's awake."

"He can walk the rest of the way to your father's house."

"I don't mind carrying him."

"Scout has you wrapped around his little paw."

"There are worst places to be."

Dakota couldn't think of one. Or another person she'd rather be spending time with.

Bryce cared enough to carry the tired dog. He'd been generous with his time to help her. He seemed uncertain around Rascal, but he hadn't let those feelings stop him from going on the walk. Those things appealed to her, and she wanted to get to know him better.

She followed him up the walkway and then stopped. "Oops. I wasn't thinking about Rascal being with us. I need to stay outside with him."

"He's on a leash. Bring him inside."

"Bad idea. Remember my dining room?"

"He wasn't being supervised."

"That was my fault." She still felt bad about what happened. "I let his good behavior sway me, and I gave him freedom before he was ready. I won't make that mistake again."

Bryce opened the front door. "Come in. Rascal, too."

Even though this could turn into a disaster of epic proportions, Dakota stepped inside. The dog followed her.

A delicious smell filled the air. She could make out the chicken, but the spices eluded her. Rosemary, perhaps?

Walt sat in his recliner. No one else was here.

Bryce closed the front door. "Where is everyone?"

"They put dinner in the oven before they left." Walt waved to Rascal, who wagged his tail. "Do you have plans for dinner, Dakota? We have enough to feed an army."

Shaking his head, Bryce glanced her way with an I-told-you-so look and then placed Scout on the ground. The dog took off running with his leash attached.

Dakota wasn't worried. The little dog couldn't outrun her though he might try. "I'd love to stay and eat. Thanks."

Scout ran toward Walt. Tiny paws clicked against the floor. The long leash dragged behind him. The dog jumped onto the arm of the recliner.

Bryce walked to the chair, although she didn't know if he was checking on his dad or the dog. "I had no idea something so small could jump so high."

"Me, either." She kept a tight hold on Rascal in case he got any ideas about getting on the chair, too. "I hope he didn't hurt you, Walt."

"This little thing?" Walt scooted over to make a space between the chair arm and him. Scout lay in the spot and rested his head on Walt's leg. "No way."

Bryce laughed. "Looks like Scout's settled in."

A satisfied smile settled on Walt's lips. "Must be worn out from his walk."

She nodded. "He fell asleep at the end."

Rascal walked toward Bryce. The leash pulled tight. Both dogs seemed to have a favorite Grayson.

That made her smile. "I'll take the dogs home. Otherwise, we'll never be able to eat in peace."

"That'll make getting your car from the feed store easier," Bryce said.

"And yours."

Walt petted Scout's head. "Promise you'll bring them back for a longer visit."

She grinned. The two looked cute together in the recliner. "I will."

Bryce picked up Scout, placed the dog on the ground, and walked him over. He handed the leash to her.

Rascal nudged toward his hand, and Bryce stiffened. Then he touched the top of the dog's head. Slowly. Tentatively.

Her throat tightened, and she swallowed.

One pet. Two. He pulled his arm to his side.

Tail wagging, Rascal seemed happy.

Dakota was. "I'll be back in a few minutes."

She headed out with two dogs. A hundred thoughts ran through her mind.

How did Bryce play into her wanting to date again? Was this just a crush, her fangirling, as Portia and Kelly had mentioned?

That would explain Dakota's feelings, her body reacting the way it did around him, and why she kept wanting to sneak glances his way. But what did crushing on Bryce mean now that she'd spent the afternoon with him and was having dinner at his house tonight?

She was getting to know Bryce, little by little. She liked him.

No denying that.

But he was just a guy, a nice guy who was kind and handsome and lived in Seattle.

Seattle, Washington.

A long way from Marietta, Montana.

What had Kelly called his leaving? A built-in end date?

Dakota might be ready to date, and dating was a long way from falling for a guy, but she still wanted to be careful.

If Bryce asked her out—and that was still a big if since he hadn't been keen on his dad's matchmaking—would she be able to keep things casual as Kelly put it? Or would Dakota be setting herself up for another failure with yet another Mr. Wrong? This one who lived a completely different life in a far-off place?

Yes, she was attracted to Bryce, but maybe the best thing would be if she waited to date until he was gone.

That would be the smartest move.

And the safest one.

She only hoped she would be smart and safe where Bryce Grayson was concerned.

Chapter Nine

SATURDAY, BRYCE FIXED breakfast for his father, but he couldn't stop thinking about Dakota. She seemed to enjoy herself yesterday. His father's smug expression had him looking like the matchmaker king—just add a crown and scepter.

Bryce liked seeing his dad so happy, so he hadn't bothered to call out his father's cupid-wannabe efforts. Dakota hadn't let on that she'd already been invited to dinner, either. His father still thought he was getting away with his making-a-match gig, but if that made him feel better, so be it.

Bryce and Dakota knew the truth. He scrambled eggs in the pan and then added grated cheese. Except...

He didn't quite know what was going on with her.

Their time together had been going great until they returned to the feed store for their cars last night. There'd been an awkward moment in the parking lot.

Bryce hadn't known what to expect—a kiss, a hug, a simple goodnight. But a handshake?

That had felt wrong. Bad. A whole lot of other things.

They hadn't been on a date, even if it felt like one, but still…

No one shook hands after having so much fun together. She seemed to forget those glances she kept sending his way or the not-so-accidental touches.

A hug would have been better than a handshake.

Bryce sprinkled salt and added a dash of pepper to the scrambled eggs.

No distractions, remember?

He should be relieved Dakota hadn't kissed him or wanted him to kiss her or any variation in between.

But Bryce wasn't relieved. If anything, he was curious, confused, and a little upset. He dished out the breakfast and carried a plate of eggs, bacon, and toast to his dad. "Here you go."

"Thanks." His dad placed his crossword puzzle on the end table. "The house is quiet this morning. Too quiet."

"This is how it always is unless you have friends over."

"Or dogs. I should say a dog." His father picked up a slice of bacon. "Scout didn't make a peep while he was here. Little guy settled in like he owned the place."

"Your recliner, anyway."

"I didn't mind. He fit perfectly." His father grinned. "Rascal could wake the dead. I swear he makes noise when he wags his tail."

"He's not that bad." At least the dog hadn't been last

night. "Just big and clumsy."

"And does the opposite of what you tell him."

Rain pelted the roof. Bryce glanced out the living room window. Dark skies and wet pavement. He hoped the storm wouldn't keep people away from the adoption event today. "Dakota said he went right in his crate at home and fell asleep."

"Exhaustion will do that to an animal or a person." A serious expression crossed his dad's face. "That's why I worry about Dakota. I don't know how she keeps up with everything. The dogs, the rat, her job, volunteering, and her house."

"She seems to be handling it all."

"I'm afraid she's going to burn out if she's not careful."

That didn't seem like the organized woman Bryce was getting to know. "You think so?"

His father nodded. "She changed after her fiancé broke up with her on their wedding day."

Bryce's chest tightened thinking how that must have hurt Dakota. "She got jilted?"

"Yes. I was in the church when she made the announcement that the wedding had been called off. Her loser of a fiancé left her to do that."

Bryce's fingers curled. He hoped Dakota was over the guy. "Loser seems like too nice a word."

"You're right since he married another woman three months later." His dad shook his head. "Dakota's never mentioned the wedding again or the guy, but since then, she's been working non-stop between her job and the rescue. I doubt she takes a day off."

That Bryce could imagine. The woman never seemed to stop.

Her work ethic appealed to him, but he wondered if the non-stop doing had become a coping mechanism for her. His job had been his sanctuary after his mother's death. Losing himself in a design project had made turning off his grief easier.

Was Dakota doing the same thing to escape her heart-ache?

That would explain how she acted around him. Some-times hot, other times cold.

He stared at the falling rain. "Is that why you keep send-ing me to wherever she is?"

"Coincidence."

Sure, it was. But no harm in letting his dad believe the matchmaking was working. "Guess that happens in a small town."

"All the time." His dad ate a forkful of eggs. "You should see if they need help at the adoption event today."

They. His dad meant Dakota. Bryce bit back a smile. "I told her to call if she needs help."

"Nice of you to offer. I hope she calls you."

"Figured that's what you would be doing if you hadn't broken your legs."

His dad shot him a pointed look. "Are you helping because of me? Or is there something going on between you and Dakota?"

"You want me to help, so I am. Nothing's going on between us. Why do you ask?"

He raised his coffee cup. "Just curious. You seem to get along well."

"We do." Bryce pictured her smiling face. "She's smart, pretty, and funny. What's not to like? But I'm not here to find a girlfriend. I'm here to spend time with you."

"You could do a lot worse than Dakota Parker."

If Bryce were in the market for a girlfriend... He shrugged.

"Ask her out on a date." The mischief in his dad's eyes matched his voice. "She's all those things you mentioned, plus she has a heart as wide as the Rockies."

Bryce couldn't believe he was having this conversation with his dad and not one about moving to Washington. "She also lives in Marietta. I live in Seattle."

"Then make the most of the time you're here."

Bryce shrugged. "She doesn't seem interested. She could still be getting over her ex-fiancé?"

"Or she's old fashioned and waiting for you to make the first move."

She'd been the one to kiss him, so Bryce didn't think that was the case. "Dakota seems the type to go after what she wants."

And from the looks of things, she didn't want him.

She hadn't used the F-word—friends—but that appeared to be what they were, but he couldn't forget her kissing him. He needed to focus on something else. "If the rain lets up, I'll drive you by your job sites."

His father perked up. "You can try out your new socks."

Bryce half-laughed. "Yes, I can."

"Maybe we could go by the feed store."

"I don't need another pair of socks," he played along.

His father's eyebrows furrowed. "To see how the adoption event is going."

"We'll see how long the rain lasts." Bryce hoped not long. The dreary weather was affecting his mood.

His dad picked up the remote and turned on the television. "I'm going to see what college football games are on."

Bryce had been so busy with the animal rescue's proposal and his dad that he hadn't been working on his own business. "I'm going to dive back into my proposal so I can have stuff to my assistant on Monday morning."

"You really want to win that big contract?" his father asked.

"Yes." Just thinking about winning brought a rush of pride and exhilaration. "It would take my firm to the next level."

"You'll be working even harder than you do now."

"That's how I pay bills and survive."

"You still need to live."

"I do."

"As fully as you could?"

"I'm trying."

His father's eyes clouded. "Your mother had so many dreams, but not many came true."

"Mom was a daydreamer. She liked talking about things rather than actually doing them."

"Part of the problem was me. If I hadn't been so focused on work, I could have done more to make her dreams come true."

"Mom knew how much your business meant to you. She loved you so much and wanted you to be happy. The same with me." Saying the words brought that funny taste back to his mouth.

"Your mother put our needs ahead of her own. Ahead of her health."

"That's the kind of person she was." Dakota was like that in some ways, but she was working toward her dream of getting animals adopted with her proposals. That made Bryce wonder what other goals she had.

"I should have thought about putting her first. Gone on the trips. Made you come home."

His throat constricted so tight only a small amount of air seemed to be able to get through. "Having regrets after you lose someone is normal, Dad."

"Yes, and the holidays coming up don't help. But what good are the regrets if you don't do something? Take some sort of action so you don't have the same ones later?"

Bryce's jaw tensed. "I wish I could go back and do over so many things with Mom. That's why I want you to move to Seattle. So we can be closer and spend more time together."

Time he'd missed with his mom for no other reason than focusing on what he'd wanted at the time—fun with his friends or then-girlfriends—rather than what his mother wanted—a holiday together or a family vacation.

"And that's the same reason I want you to stay in Marietta." His father's gaze bore into Bryce. "The pace is slower than what you're used to, but you could marry a nice woman like Dakota and raise a family. You could be happy here and have a good life."

No wonder his dad was playing matchmaker. He wanted Bryce to stay in Marietta, but in spite of his father's intentions, that wasn't going to happen. "I have a good life where I am."

"If you say so." His dad didn't sound convinced. "But think about it."

"I will." Bryce would. He owed his dad that.

"Think about asking Dakota out, too."

Bryce laughed. "You're not going to give up on that one, are you?"

"Nope."

"I'll think about that, too."

But no way did Dakota Parker play into his future. Not

the one his father imagined for him in Marietta or the one Bryce saw for himself in Seattle.

SUNDAY MORNING AT the feed store, Dakota tried to keep her nervous energy under wraps. She held Scout on her lap. She placed the bright yellow "Adopt Me" vest on his back, clasped the buckle underneath his belly, and then attached the strap around his chest. A symphony of meows sounded from the cats, but Scout stood still as if he knew what was at stake.

She checked the two buckles to make sure they weren't too tight or loose. "You'll find your family soon, little guy."

Scout stared up at her.

She touched his head. "You are too cute."

But his eyes seemed those of an old soul, not an almost seven-year-old dog. Maybe that was why Scout had seemed so comfortable with Walt on Friday night. Walt had the same look in his eyes.

Not Bryce. Or maybe that baby blue color mesmerized her so she couldn't see anything else. He hadn't stopped by yesterday. She'd half-expected Walt to send him on another errand for a pack of seeds or something, and she'd been disappointed when Bryce hadn't shown.

Silly. She barely knew him and couldn't even call him a friend. Guess she was crushing on him.

Veronica, one of today's volunteers, wore her Whiskers

and Paw Pals T-shirt. She secured a blue vest on one of the other dogs up for adoption. "Thank goodness the rain stopped. Do you think the weather affected the turnout yesterday?"

"Hard to say." Dakota glanced to the double glass doors. Yesterday, they'd been able to see the rain coming down outside, but people had still dropped by. They needed heavier traffic today. "Two dogs and five cats found forever homes. I hope drier skies mean more animals will find homes today."

"I've told everyone who's come into the clinic to come see the animals. So has Kelly."

"Appreciate that."

The Copper Mountain Animal Hospital was a big supporter of Whiskers and Paw Pals. They also were the main medical provider. Dakota hoped word of mouth and social media would be enough to bring in potential adopters.

She crossed her fingers. Not much else she could do at this point, though Lori was being interviewed on a radio program this morning to try to get more publicity for the adoption drive.

Maybe the thought of displaced shelter animals would tug on heartstrings. That was all they had going for them right now. Although, Lori had approved of the changes to the *Home for Thanksgiving* proposal. She would present the plan to the board of directors as soon as they heard from the benefactor. Unfortunately, no one knew when that would be.

But not knowing didn't lessen the pressure to find adopters. These fur babies needed homes.

A dog barked—Rascal. This was his first adoption event. Yesterday, he'd been restless. She had a feeling today would be the same.

Other dogs joined in, including Hank, the feed store's hound dog who'd been adopted from the rescue two years ago. He was the store's mascot and appeared in their ads.

Dakota had to laugh. "Looks like the day has begun."

"It's going to be a loud one." Kelly checked the vests and leashes on each dog. "Hey, the boss is here."

What? Lori was supposed to be doing the radio broadcast.

Dakota glanced toward the door. Sage, the owner of Copper Mountain Chocolates, walked in. She wore jeans, rain boots, and a tan parka. Her long, red hair and golden complexion looked gorgeous as usual.

Sage carried something covered with a large plastic bag. "Good morning."

"Hey." Dakota hoped nothing was wrong at the chocolate shop. She handed Scout's leash to Kelly and walked over to her boss. "I didn't expect to see you here this morning."

"Portia mentioned what you'd taken on at the rescue. I want to help."

"That's so nice of you."

Sage pulled out a basket full of small chocolate paws

wrapped in cellophane and tied with brightly colored ribbons. "Dawson took the kids to the park yesterday, so I went into the shop to start on holiday items. I had leftover chocolate, so I thought I'd try some new molds before I left." She handed over the basket. "Rosie and Portia packaged them for me."

"This is such a surprise."

Her boss's generosity brought tears to Dakota's eyes. Some people wondered why she chose to work at a chocolate shop—part time no less. Working for Sage was a big reason. Another was she loved the job. She didn't have any frustrations over feeling incompetent or slow to catch on. She didn't need the money, but the salary covered her meager expenses, and she was free to volunteer as much as she wanted. A fancy title and big paycheck had never been as important to her as being happy and being home.

"They're adorable," Dakota added. "Thank you so much."

"Least I can do after all you do." Sage looked around. Her eyes widened. "Look at all the animals."

"I'm hoping many potential adopters show up."

"Me, too." Sage smiled warmly. "Give these chocolate paws away or sell them. Whatever you think will best help the animals.

"Will do." Dakota stared at the paws with gratitude in her heart. Maybe this was a sign today would be awesome. "I hope you have a great day."

"I hope yours is better. Good luck finding forever homes for the animals."

As Sage spoke to friends and feed shop customers, Dakota handed the basket to today's social media person, a young woman named Amie, who'd volunteered the night of the water damage to help out. "Take a picture of the basket and get the word out that we have chocolate paws made by Copper Mountain Chocolates."

"How much are we selling them for?" Amie asked.

Dakota rubbed her face. Bringing more people to the feed store was the goal today, not fundraising. She hoped Lori agreed. "Free, but mention donations gratefully accepted."

"I'm on it."

She glanced at her cell phone. Almost time.

Excitement nearly conquered her nerves. She clapped her hands to get the volunteers' attention. "Let's get the dogs in place and show off these wonderful fur babies."

Please, adopters. Come today.

Rascal kicked off the official event with a series of sharp barks, but Dakota managed to quiet him.

Everyone stared at the door, including the dogs. Waiting. Hoping.

Nerves gave way to panic. Dakota wrung her hands.

Kelly flashed a reassuring smile. "They'll come."

Dakota nodded, but her insides twisted.

The door opened, and a family of five walked in.

She blew out a puff of air. Maybe today wouldn't be a disaster.

People trickled in. Slow at first, but more than yesterday. Whether the sunshine or the free chocolate paws brought them to the feed shop, Dakota didn't care. Dogs and cats were getting attention from customers, potential adopters, friends, and chocolate lovers. Some people were ready to fill out paperwork to be approved. Others wanted more information and time to decide.

Dakota answered questions. Finding homes was the goal, but only if the combination was a good fit for all involved—humans and animals.

Dogs barked and showed off for people. Some cats put on a show in their crates, but others slept. A typical adoption event, but a solid kick-off—albeit an informal one—could spur the ones that followed.

A man, woman, and three children, ranging in age from six to twelve, approached.

Dakota recognized them from the chocolate shop. The man taught math at the high school. "Hello. Did you get a chocolate paw?"

The woman nodded. "Yes, and we'd like to find out what we have to do to adopt the white poodle named Molly."

The words filled Dakota with joy. "Molly is a sweetheart. She loves children."

"We love her," the youngest, a girl with her hair French

braided, said.

The other four nodded.

The anticipation in their eyes matched Dakota's. She wiggled her toes inside her boots and handed the woman a clipboard. "The first step to Molly joining your family is filling out this form. After that, one of our adoption counselors will review the information with you."

They did. The entire time the three kids each kept a hand on Molly, and the dog soaked up the attention. After a call was made to the adopter's veterinary reference, Molly was officially adopted.

Dakota touched the poodle. "Enjoy your new home, beautiful."

More adoptions followed.

Pixel, a black cat who looked like a miniature panther, was adopted next by a family with two teens who'd lost their fifteen-year-old cat to renal failure two months ago. They'd been pre-approved by the rescue to adopt, but they'd been waiting for the right time. That turned out to be today.

A family fell in love with Bodie, the Patterdale Terrier, and a young couple adopted two cats, the calico Jinx and the gray Crystal.

"It's going well. The chocolate paws are a big hit." Kelly stationed herself by the cats, but she kept an eye on the dogs, too. The vet tech watched out for all the animals. "Happy?"

"Yes, but I want more," Dakota admitted. "Is that wrong?"

"Not wrong. Human." Kelly smiled. "We're just getting going. It'll happen."

Dakota hoped so.

Bettina Andrews entered the feed shop. A wide smile lit up her face. She was a retired fourth grade teacher and was greeted by former students of all ages. "Where are those chocolate paws I saw on the Internet?"

"Over here, Mrs. Andrews." Dakota motioned to the table with the basket of chocolates and brochures. "Help yourself."

Mrs. Andrews took three paws from the basket and put a five-dollar bill in the jar marked *donations*. "I have two dogs at home, but I want to support the rescue. You do good work."

"Thank you," Dakota said to the older woman. "We appreciate your support. This truly is a community effort."

"Happy to help." She looked over at the dogs. Her lips parted. "Oh, look at that big yellow one over there."

Dakota followed the woman's line of sight. "That's River Jack. He's one of our Lonely Heart dogs. Been here a while, but that's given him more time to lose weight. As you can see, he still has more to go."

Mrs. Andrews took a step toward the dog and then stopped. She looked back at Dakota. "Is it okay if I pet him?"

"Please feel free. River Jack loves rubs almost as much as he loves food."

She laughed. "So do I."

River Jack was on his feet by the time Mrs. Andrews reached him. He nudged her hand with his muzzle, a sign he wanted her to pet him.

Mrs. Andrews sighed. "What a sweetheart. How long has he been at the rescue?"

"Over a year. He was found down by the river. That's why he's named River Jack."

"If he's been here that long, it means he missed a birthday."

"Dr. Sullivan estimates River Jack to be seven or eight years old."

"He's a handsome fellow." Her gaze never left the dog. "I only came for the chocolate paws, but…"

River Jack pressed against Mrs. Andrews.

"Oh, dear. You're a doll, aren't you?" she said to him. "We're planning to go to Florida this winter to be with our daughter. I really shouldn't, but… Oh, I can't resist his face. Our son, Jonah, will be staying at our house with the dogs. What's one more?"

Dakota could barely breathe. Finding a home for River Jack—or any of the Lonely Heart animals—would be incredible. "You said you have two dogs."

"Sweethearts, both of them." Mrs. Andrews didn't let go of River Jack. "One is a Beagle and the other is a chow mix who belonged to our younger son."

River Jack got along well with other dogs at the rescue.

Dakota wanted to make sure this was a good fit.

"Do you want to have your husband bring your dogs over here, just to make sure everyone gets along?"

That way she could also make sure Mr. Andrews agreed with his wife's decision to adopt. That sometimes wasn't the case.

"A wonderful idea. Though I'm sure he'll say 'Betts, have you lost your mind?'" Mrs. Andrews beamed. "Kelly over there works at the vet where we go, so she can help with the dog introduction."

Dakota nodded. "That sounds like a wonderful idea."

Less than an hour later, River Jack was on his way to the Andrews' house. Two more cats, Gabby and Sinclair, found families and so did dogs Dobie and Casper.

Dakota couldn't believe how well the event was going. She rose up on her tiptoes. "Could this day get any better?"

"There's still plenty of time left to find out."

Bryce. His voice gave her chills—the good kind.

She turned around and hugged him. His fresh scent surrounded her, and his warm body was furnace hot. "River Jack got adopted."

He wrapped his arms around her waist. "I have no idea who that is, but if you're happy, I am, too."

Oops. Maybe that was a bit too enthusiastic of a greeting.

She let go and stepped back to put distance between them. Immediately, she missed having him so close. "River

Jack's been at the rescue a long time. Too long. Your dad knows all about him."

"Good for River Jack. And good for you. I'll tell my dad."

The event area was packed with people looking at animals. She checked the time. "What are you doing here so early?"

"Willa challenged my dad to a cribbage duel, so he told me I could go. Suggested I stop by here to say hi and lend a hand."

Dakota laughed.

"Need help with anything?" he asked.

"Yes, please. Rascal's been barking. He's having a rough time settling down with so many people and other animals around. Could you please take him outside where it's quieter?"

Bryce's face paled.

Oh, right. He wasn't comfortable with the puppy. "Never mind. I'll find someone else."

"No, it's fine." His voice sounded tight. "I just have to hold his leash, right?"

"Yes, but you might need a tight grip."

The corners of his lips tipped upward. "I have one of those."

She remembered his strong hands keeping her steady. Her temperature rose, and she fought the urge to fan herself.

"I know." Her voice sounded deeper than normal. "But,

if you'd rather not—"

"I've got this."

"Okay. Just remember, you're in charge. Not the other way around."

A volunteer handed Dakota a completed cat application.

One more animal who found a home. With a heart feeling as light as a feather, she looked at Bryce. "I need to take care of this."

"Go ahead." He dragged his teeth over his lower lip. "Rascal and I will figure this out."

Dakota hesitated. "As long as you're sure."

"I am." He sounded confident.

Rascal would never hurt anyone, even though that deep, sharp bark suggested otherwise. But probably the less she said, the better.

Maybe this was the start of a new friendship between the two. She hoped so, but she only wished the sound of something happening between her and Bryce didn't appeal to her so much.

Chapter Ten

T HE ADOPTION EVENT ended with smiles and cheers on Sunday afternoon. Bryce had managed to control Rascal, and the two had reached an understanding—Bryce would pet the dog if the puppy behaved. That had worked well, although his hand was tired.

Bryce loaded the final table into a volunteer's minivan. An older woman named Veronica was going to store them until the rescue was back up and running, which shouldn't be long. A construction crew had begun repairs. He walked back inside.

Dakota was speaking to Tim, the feed store owner. She handed him a bag from Copper Mountain Chocolates.

Neither Scout nor Rascal had been adopted and would be going home with Dakota. He glanced at the two dogs in their crates. "She's something else."

Rascal barked.

The beast seemed to agree. The dog listened better than people thought.

With a wide smile on her face. Dakota walked toward

him with a slight bounce to her step. "Eleven adoptions today, seven from yesterday, and two in Bozeman, including Maverick."

"Which one is Maverick?" he asked.

"The sad Border Collie from the parking lot. He used to live on a ranch and was adopted by a cattle rancher. My friend Janie says it's a perfect fit. I couldn't be more pleased. Maverick is an awesome herder and a real love."

Bryce remembered. She'd been kneeling in front of the crate of the whimpering dog. "So how many adoptions does that make?"

"Twenty." Dakota's brown eyes sparkled. "I can't believe it."

"I can. You and all the volunteers worked hard."

"We have so much more to do."

"Not tonight," he said. "Twenty adoptions deserve a celebration."

"True. I wish I could celebrate. I'm sure the others will." She didn't sound upset, only tired. "Pierre has been alone for the past two days, and I want to spend time with him. I also need to figure out how I'm going to canvas the town tomorrow to let them know about the *Home for Thanksgiving* program if it's approved by the board."

"You have to eat."

"I will."

His dad was correct. She worked too hard. Bryce wanted to make sure she ate after being on her feet for two days.

"How about I grab a pizza and swing by your place?" he asked. "You like pepperoni, right?

Her nose scrunched. "I do, but shouldn't you be home with your dad?"

"His friends are over. And he'll be pleased we're spending time together."

She shook her head. "You're going to make him think his matchmaking is working."

Bryce shrugged. "It makes him happy."

She hesitated. "Pizza does sound good."

"Great." And it was. Something about Dakota brought out his protective instincts. She was fully capable of taking care of everything herself, but having someone to look after her might help. "I'll head over there now before the wait gets too long."

"See you soon," she said.

"Me, too. I expect a tour of the house."

She laughed. "So you have an ulterior motive for coming over."

Did he? "Maybe so."

FORTY-FIVE MINUTES LATER, Bryce knocked on Dakota's front door. He heard barks. Rascal.

Dakota opened the door. Pierre, the gray rat with big ears, sat on her shoulder. "That was fast."

"No wait for the pizza." He'd made good time at the

convenience market, too. So they could eat, not because he wanted to see her. Rather, her house. "Pierre looks comfortable."

"This is his favorite spot."

Bryce didn't blame the rat for wanting to be with Dakota. He didn't get the appeal of a rodent for a pet, but this one looked harmless. Pierre's whiskers twitched, but his eyes weren't that beady.

"Where's Rascal? I need to know if I should prepare myself for a pounce."

"He's in his crate. Scout, too. They both had two long days."

So had Dakota. She was smiling, but the circles under her eyes told him the weekend was catching up with her.

"You brought more than pizza," she said.

"Salad and breadsticks." He raised the bag in his left hand. "And to celebrate the twenty adoptions, I picked up a bottle of red wine and a six-pack of beer. I wasn't sure which you preferred."

She motioned him inside. "That was sweet of you. Thanks."

As soon as he entered the house, barks erupted. "Do they have some kind of radar?"

"A territorial kind that works better than an alarm system. No batteries or electricity required."

She walked past the staircase on her right and the living room on her left. "The kitchen is in the back. I eat in there so the animals can have the dining room, though I some-times work in there."

He remembered the papers and books. "Have you always used the dining room for your foster animals?"

"I started doing that after my great aunt died. The dining room has easy access to the back door in the kitchen. The large windows bring in natural light, and the animals can see outside. I have a room upstairs that I use to quarantine a new foster, and then they join the menagerie down here."

"Sounds like it works well."

She nodded. "I don't entertain much, and my family is so spread out I don't need a formal dining room. The kitchen table works fine."

"You're not the only one who feels that way. Open floor plans with only one dining area are the trend right now. Few ask for formal living or dining room."

Rascal saw him and barked.

Dakota raised a finger, and the dog didn't bark again.

No rubs required. Bryce was impressed. "He's learning."

"Rascal knows the commands. Whether he follows them is the problem." She entered the kitchen. "Welcome to the first remodeling mess of the evening."

He stopped in the doorway. Two adjectives came to mind—ugly and wasted space. He could look beyond color and style. Those were easy fixes. But what this kitchen needed wasn't going to be an easy change.

The stove was positioned completely wrong. The refrigerator was by the table, not anywhere near the counter space or sink. The cabinets didn't reach the ceiling, but the space above was too narrow to be used for storage or decorations.

He couldn't see one redeeming feature other than it was clean, and he'd worked on many kitchens in his day. "I don't know what to say."

"Horrible doesn't begin to describe this kitchen." She touched a magnet-covered refrigerator that made funny noises. It had to be thirty-years old. "The worst part is my great aunt and uncle contributed to this mess by adding in the fake woodgrain countertop and the log cabin wallpaper after they moved in."

The appliance placement and mix match of styles and color schemes made Bryce's teeth hurt. "This needs to be gutted so you can start over."

"That's why I haven't touched this room. The appliances work, and there's space to prepare meals so no rush when we need to start from scratch."

Bryce understood due to the logistics and finances involved. Kitchen renovations were difficult on homeowners, but he disagreed from a matter of aesthetics.

"You're the one who has to live here."

"I just don't want to get too used to it."

He smiled. "I don't think that'll be a problem."

Bryce looked beyond the cosmetics to the dimension and placement of the walls, doorways and windows. He stared at the wall separating the kitchen and dining room. "If this wall isn't load bearing, you could open this up and change the entire feel."

She grinned. "Looks like I know who to call for ideas when I'm ready to remodel the kitchen."

"I'll be in Seattle by then, but I'll leave notes with my dad." The thought of not being here to see what she did bothered him more than it should. He raised the bag in his hand. "Where do you want the food?"

"On the counter." She touched Pierre. "I'm going to put him away. You've got a few minutes if you want to take a quick look at the rest of the house."

That was trusting of her. Or maybe that was how people who lived in small towns acted. Or how she treated friends.

"Anything off-limits?" he asked.

"Just my underwear drawer." She grinned.

That made him wonder if she preferred lacy underwear to plain cotton. With a shake of his head, he set off on his tour.

A door near the dining room was ajar, so he looked inside.

The bathroom had a harvest gold tub and toilet with a gold-veined shell-shaped sink and countertop. Given the style, this was likely remodeled in the 1980s.

Bryce walked toward the entryway. The living room was now on his right. He peeked inside. A nice-sized white brick fireplace with built-in shelves on either side was the focal point of the room. In spite of the three windows along one side, the large space seemed cave-like and gave off a 1990s vibe.

He climbed the stairs. The bannister looked original. Sanding and stain would go a long way.

Framed photographs hung on the wall in a haphazard array. One showed a young family of five near the Spanish Steps in Rome. Another shot had them standing with the Seattle Space Needle in the background.

Bryce wanted to take his dad there. Pike Place Market, too, and a hundred other places. His dad would never be bored living in Seattle.

Picking out Dakota in the pictures was easy. Her smile hadn't changed. She was a cute kid who seemed to like pigtails and baseball caps when she was younger.

He went up to the second floor to a small landing. A cat tree sat in the corner, but he saw no cats. She must foster those, too.

The first door on the left led to a bathroom. He shook his head. Turquoise and yellow tiles covered the floors and walls. The toilet and bathtub were turquoise, too. Circa 1950s, he guessed. Although older than the downstairs bathroom, this one appeared in better shape.

The three upstairs bedrooms had been painted white. Only one looked occupied with an overstuffed chair and ottoman in one corner and a queen-sized sleigh bed against the wall with matching nightstands and a dresser. The patchwork quilt on the bed was homey looking. The room was comfortable, feminine but not too frilly.

Dakota's room?

Most likely. The other two had beds, but nothing to make them seem lived in like this one. He headed toward the stairs.

Dakota was halfway up them. "Dinner's on the table."

"Great house. Solid with so many possibilities."

His mind was spinning with ideas. Removing walls on both floors would make the house more open and livable. Adding a master bathroom to her bedroom would add equity. But this wasn't his project.

"You're going to have fun remodeling this place," he added.

"It's been interesting, so far."

Bryce motioned to the photographs on the wall. "Nice family."

"My mom loves to take pictures." Dakota pointed to a teenager. "This is my brother York when he was in high school. He's a computer whiz in the Air Force. The little girl next to him is my younger sister Nevada. She's getting her PhD right now and wants to be a college professor."

"Did you ever want to go to grad school?"

"My mom was pushing me toward law school. She still is, but college was hard enough. The idea of law school doesn't appeal to me at all. If I had to get a nine-to-five type job, I'd rather work in animal advocacy or a lobby group. Something where I could make a difference."

"You're making a difference now."

"Thank you. I just wish my mother could see that. She's so proud of my siblings, but she thinks I'm throwing away my degree working in a chocolate shop and volunteering. But I'm happy, and one of these days, the opportunity to do more will come along."

"Or you'll decide to make your own opportunity."

"That, too."

"York, Nevada, and Dakota." Bryce repeated the three names. "Your parents must be geography buffs."

"We moved all the time, so I always thought they named us after the places they'd lived, but my dad was never stationed in New York or in England. York jokes that our names are the places we were conceived, but my parents have neither confirmed nor denied that."

The Parker family sounded interesting. "Where do your parents live?"

"On a sailboat." She pointed to another picture that showed a fit couple in their fifties on a sandy beach with palm trees behind them. "After my dad retired two years ago, they purchased a boat and sailed south. Right now, I think they're in Belize."

"You think? Don't you worry about them being so far away?"

She shrugged. "I wish I saw them more, especially during the holidays, but my parents are living their dream. I'm happy they're able to do that after a life full of military deployments, moves, and other sacrifices."

Bryce could understand that, but his dad wasn't living his dream in Marietta. He was living out his late wife's dream. He'd been here three years. This had to be some kind of phase. One that was time to end.

"I'm having a hard enough time with my dad in Montana. No way would I want him to live in another country."

"Your dad is awesome. He's so happy you're here this month."

That was good to know. They would have more time together in Seattle. He just needed to get his father to see that.

"It's great being here with him." Bryce studied more pictures. None showed Dakota with men other than her father and brother. "My dad's always wanted a personal minion to do his bidding. Now he has me."

She laughed. "Maybe that's why your father seems…more content…even with two broken legs. That's your doing."

"I worry he's lonely."

"Living alone takes some getting used to, but he's got you now."

"I'll be leaving a couple of days after Thanksgiving. I have to get back to work."

And turn in his proposal. He'd then be waiting to hear if he was invited to make a presentation.

Bryce thought about telling Dakota how much he wanted his father to move to Seattle but decided against it. He didn't want to spoil tonight, and it might because Dakota valued his father's advice. The two shared a close friendship. She wouldn't want Walt to move away, even if it were to be closer to Bryce.

He took a step down. "We should eat before the pizza gets cold."

ON MONDAY, DAKOTA put an *adopt me* vest on Scout and walked around Main Street. Inside her backpack were promotion packets—a flier to hang on windows or community bulletin boards, information cards, and brochures—about the *Home for Thanksgiving* Adoption Drive.

She'd been careful about what she'd asked for from the employees and volunteers at the rescue who took care of marketing materials. She wanted to make sure what was printed could be used whether the benefactor came through or the proposal was accepted by the board. All she needed was the call from Lori to proceed, but at least people were seeing one of the available animals.

Staying home and resting on her day off probably would have been better, but she needed to stay busy. Otherwise, she kept thinking about Bryce. The man had even invaded her dreams last night.

Pent-up frustration, according to Kelly when they'd spoke earlier.

Maybe that was it.

They'd enjoyed a nice dinner, never ran out of things to discuss, and he'd even helped with the dishes. But when the time came for him to leave, the only thing they exchanged was a "goodnight."

Her lips had been screaming in protest, but she hadn't felt like making a move. After he'd mentioned going back to Seattle, shaking hands again hadn't appealed to her, even though she'd wanted to touch him.

Had his words been a warning? Or just what was going to happen? She had no idea, but she'd taken his words as a sign not to get too close.

Her cell phone beeped.

Maddie Cash's name and number appeared on the screen.

Maddie: *Sorry I couldn't get Clementine to the adoption event this weekend.*

Maddie: *I had open houses both days.*

Dakota: *That's okay. We're having another this weekend. The rescue might be back open by then, too.*

Maddie: *Keep me posted.*

Dakota: *Will do.*

She tucked her phone away.

Time to pay a visit to the next shop on her list—the flower shop. All the pretty blossoms in the buckets outside made her want to splurge on a bouquet.

Why not?

As Bryce said, twenty adoptions deserved a celebration. More than one.

She reached for the doorknob. The ringtone *Who Let the Dogs Out* played. Lori. The flowers would have to wait.

Had the director received an answer from the benefactor?

Dakota's heart lodged in her throat. She pulled out her phone and placed it at her ear. "Hey."

"It's a go."

"Which part?"

"All of it. I heard from the benefactor and just left the board meeting."

"What?" The word was whisper-quiet. That was all she could muster with her mind racing.

"The benefactor said any dog in a foster-to-adopt program or in a fospice situation is exempt."

Dakota blew out a breath. "What about the Lonely Hearts and dogs who aren't quite ready, like Rascal?"

"They count, but that's less than a dozen, right?"

"Less than half a dozen, but still…"

"We can do this, so get canvassing and putting *Home for Thanksgiving* into action. I need to run by the rescue and talk to the contractor. We'll talk later."

Lori disconnected from the call before Dakota could say goodbye.

It's a go.

Dakota couldn't believe it. She looked at Scout. "We

need to start passing out the packets, and then I can buy my flowers."

There was even more to celebrate now.

Unless, of course, this blew up in her face and she failed.

Don't think about that happening.

But there was someone she wanted to tell. She pulled up her contacts and hit G. Bryce's name was there, and though he was the first person she'd thought about calling, there was someone she needed to call instead.

She hit Walt's number.

He answered after the first ring. "Hello?"

"It's Dakota." Her emotions ping-ponged between excitement and dread. "You're never going to believe what's happened."

Chapter Eleven

T UESDAY AFTERNOON, BRYCE found himself standing on
the sidewalk outside Copper Mountain Chocolates. His
father had sent him to buy more. Another one of his mis-
guiding matchmaking attempts, but this time, Bryce was
happy to oblige. He hadn't heard from Dakota since Sunday.
He wanted to see how she was doing because he missed her.

A flyer for an upcoming Whisker and Paw Pals adoption
event this weekend hung on the shop's window. Dakota and
the rescue were going all out to try to find the animals homes
and get the donation.

He didn't know much about philanthropy and signifi-
cant donations, but this whole situation bothered him. Yes,
the benefactor had been willing to compromise on the
adoption goal, but the whole pledge felt fake. Maybe Bryce
was being cynical. Or protective of Dakota since she'd
seemed afraid of failing. Succeeding might give her the
confidence to pursue other dreams, not just ones for the
rescue, but also ones she had for herself.

He opened the door.

A familiar jingle sounded. Three, two, one…

"Welcome to Copper Mountain Chocolates."

He stiffened. That wasn't Dakota's voice. He looked to his left.

The young woman behind the counter wore a ponytail, an indigo-blue T-shirt and copper apron, and an eager smile. She'd been here last week before going into the back.

"Hello." He searched the small shop for Dakota. Not there. He ignored the twinge of disappointment. Maybe she was in the back.

"You're becoming a regular," the salesclerk said with a smile.

A regular was better than a stalker. "My father is Walt Grayson. He's addicted to your chocolate."

The young woman's smile widened. "Walt is one of the first people I met when I arrived in town. He's here almost every day. Or was until his accident. How's his recovery going?"

"Good, but he needs more chocolate to feel better." Bryce handed her his phone. "Here's his list."

"Thanks. A list will make my job easy." She grabbed a bag. "Would you like a sample and a hot chocolate while you wait?"

"No, thanks." The black-and-white photographs hanging on the wall caught his gaze. They showed how chocolate was processed in an interesting and artistic way. Whoever captured the images had talent. "I'll just look around."

The shop was cramped with four tables for customers and various displays, but everything blended nicely. Natural colors for natural products. Subtle. Nothing blaring or out of place. The designers knew what they were doing.

"I have your chocolates," the salesclerk said. "Is there anything else you'd like?"

He hesitated. Might as well ask. "Is Dakota here?"

"She's in the back." The woman rang up his purchase. "Would you like me to get her?"

He handed over his credit card. "If she's not busy."

She gave him a receipt to sign. "I'll go see if she's free."

Bryce put a five-dollar bill into the tip jar on the counter and picked up the bag. "Thanks."

Waiting, he studied the far wall and then glanced back at the retail counter. That back wall offered the perfect place to expand, if the other side was vacant. Ideas exploded in his mind. The maple display shelves would disappear, but those could be added in the new addition. The retail counter and display case on this side of the shop wouldn't have to be touched. But maybe the shop's owner wanted this store to be small and no changes were necessary.

"Bryce?"

He turned at the sound of Dakota's voice. Seeing her brought a rush of warmth. "Hey, my dad wanted more chocolate. Thought I'd say hi."

"Hi." Her hair was pulled back in a single French braid, and her smile lit up her face. Chocolate stained the lower part of her apron. "He's still matchmaking."

"I fear him and his lady friends are in cahoots."

"You're a good son."

"Trying to be." But Bryce needed to do better. "You have another adoption event this weekend?"

She nodded. "It'll be like this until Thanksgiving."

"My dad wants me to help."

"You have your proposal to work on."

Bryce was surprised she remembered. "I'm making good progress. I'd like to help."

"That would be great. I'll text you the info."

"Sounds good." Except he didn't want to wait days to see her again. Asking her out on a date was exactly what his dad wanted him to do, but Bryce knew something else they could do together. "If you want help walking the dogs after work, my dad is having dinner with people from church so I'll have free time."

"Rascal would like that."

Would she? Bryce wanted to know. "What time should I come over?"

"I'm speaking with a potential adopter at five-fifteen, so would six work?"

He nodded. "See you then. I hope the beast is happy to see me."

Bryce hoped Dakota would be happy, too.

FOR THREE NIGHTS in a row, Dakota walked the dogs with Bryce. That first night, Tuesday, they'd made specific plans, but on Wednesday and Thursday, he'd just shown up at the chocolate shop at closing time and walked home with her. That made her happy in more ways than one.

The best part was seeing him become more comfortable around Rascal. A sudden bark or movement still made Bryce stiffen, but he recovered quickly. Rascal loved walking with Bryce on the other end of the leash. The two of them would run ahead and then return to her and Scout.

But walking dogs was all they did.

Oh, they occasionally touched each other. Accidently. Although twice, Dakota had brushed him on purpose. That had led to a rush of guilt. Feelings for him kept building and growing, yet they were firmly entrenched in the friend zone without ever calling themselves friends. But what else were two adults who hung out but didn't kiss?

She wanted another kiss—make that two kisses.

Not going to happen.

On Friday, Bryce helped her set up for the weekend adoption event, and then he spent two days volunteering there. Not because of her, but for his father. Walt continued to push them together every way he could. He even watched Pierre on Saturday and Sunday, so the rat wouldn't be alone.

Rascal and Scout hadn't been adopted, but seventeen other animals found forever homes. Not as many as last weekend, but four temporary foster families decided to adopt their charges, including real estate agent Maddie Cash who couldn't bear to part with the cute Clementine.

That brought the adoption total to forty-one.

A record in two weekends?

Dakota would have to ask Lori. The repairs had been completed, and the remaining animals were moving back in this week.

With everything going so well with the *Home for Thanksgiving* adoption program, nothing else should matter, but she kept thinking about Bryce.

And thinking.

And thinking.

Last night, he'd stopped by her house to walk the dogs again. Would this continue each night? She hoped so.

On Tuesday afternoon, Dakota stood behind the counter at the chocolate shop and put together an order of mixed chocolates for the Bar V5 Dude Ranch. The housekeeping staff at the ranch placed a chocolate on their guest's pillows each night.

For the first time all day, no customers were in the shop. Dakota relished the quiet. Normally, she thrived when things were busy, but she enjoyed this break.

Portia wiped off the tables and chairs. "I can't believe I missed seeing my aunt today."

"Sage had to be at Savannah's school for a meeting so she left an hour earlier." Dakota added more chocolates to the box. "She asked me about the November event. She wants to start selling tickets."

"I've been thinking about it. The *Dark Magic Chocolate and Wine Tasting* was so fun. I loved dressing up in a costume," Portia said of last month's Halloween event at the shop. "Nothing Thanksgiving-themed, however, is calling out to me."

Dakota sighed. "Thanksgiving doesn't exactly bring to mind chocolate candy. I've been trying to think of something other than molded turkey and pilgrim hat chocolates. Though it's hard to concentrate on anything other than rescue animals and adoptions right now."

And Bryce, but that was better left unsaid. Both Portia and Sage had been asking questions about Walt's son. Rosie would be joining in if she hadn't cut back her shifts.

"You have a lot riding on that."

"Not just me." Bryce believed Dakota would succeed with the adoptions. That gave her a big boost of confidence, but at times, she wasn't sure she could pull this off. "The entire rescue shelter needs this to go well. I don't want to disappoint anyone."

Portia grinned. "A good thing you have Bryce to relieve some of the pressure."

Heat crept up Dakota's neck. "It's not like that."

"Not yet anyway." Portia's smile hinted at what might be coming.

"So the event." Dakota wanted to change the subject. "We need to get this on the calendar."

Portia dropped the rag in to the bucket. "We'll have to figure this out now."

She walked around the shop, examining each display from the glass case to the window to the shelves along the far wall.

Her lips formed a perfect O. "What if?"

Dakota straightened. "I'm listening…"

"*Make Your Own Chocolate Cornucopia* night," Portia announced. "I watched Sage put some together. People could do that and then fill them with their choice of chocolates."

Dakota could visualize the event. There wasn't much space in the shop, but if they moved the display racks, brought in tall tables where people could stand, it would work. "I like that idea, but we need something else for people to do similar to the wine tasting."

"Are there any businesses we can team up with like we did with the Two Old Goats Wine Shop?"

Dakota tapped her chin. Thanksgiving meant turkey, stuffing, cranberry sauce, and pie. That was it.

P-I-E.

And she bet that was something Bryce might eat since he didn't like chocolate. "We could talk to Rachel Vaughn over at the Gingerbread and Dessert Factory and see if she'd let Sara Maria make pies for a tasting."

"Apple, pecan, pumpkin." Excitement filled Portia's voice. "Pie would fit the Thanksgiving theme."

Dakota nodded. "Maybe once people determine their

favorites, they could pre-order their Thanksgiving pies at the tasting. We'd have to talk to Rachel about that, too."

"That would be great. I can't imagine she wouldn't want pre-orders." Portia shimmied her shoulders. "Who doesn't love pie?"

"I do."

"What about Bryce? I've never seen him take a chocolate sample. Does he have allergies or something?"

"He doesn't like chocolate."

Portia gasped. "Who doesn't like chocolate?"

Dakota shrugged.

"Then it's a good thing you're not dating him."

She nodded, but not enthusiastically.

Portia's lips parted. "I have another idea for the event. What if we buy Thanksgiving and autumn-themed decorator picks and coordinating ribbon from the craft store in Bozeman? People can decorate the box to give the cornucopia as a hostess gift, if they wanted."

"Any more ideas?" Dakota asked. "Because you are coming up with brilliant ones."

If only things at the rescue were so easy to figure out.

Portia beamed. "Let's hope my aunt agrees."

"How can she not?"

"I..." Portia glanced out the front door. The blood drained from her face. Ghost pale, she backed toward the kitchen. "If the guy across the street comes into the shop, please tell him I'm not here. Please."

She ran into the kitchen. Another door—the back door?—opened and closed.

"Portia?"

No answer.

Dakota looked in the kitchen, but she didn't see Portia. The bathroom door was open and the light off. Portia's cubby, where her personal items were kept while she worked, contained her purse. Her jacket still hung on the coat rack.

Why would she take off like that?

Dakota dialed Portia's cell phone. A ring sounded in the cubby.

Not good.

The bell on the door jingled. Dakota hurried back into the retail area.

She had no idea what was going on with Portia, but she also had a job to do. "Welcome to Copper Mountain Chocolates."

A young man closed the door behind him. Tall and thin, he wore scuffed boots, faded jeans, a long-sleeved shirt under a jean jacket, and a cowboy hat. He carried a gorgeous bouquet of flowers.

Scanning the shop, he removed his hat with his free hand. "Good day, miss."

"May I help you?" she asked.

Gaze narrowing, he surveyed the shop. The corners of his mouth turned down. "I'm Austin Bradshaw."

Portia's ex-boyfriend was named Austin. Was this him?

A hundred different scenarios spun through Dakota's mind, but she kept her smile in place. "I'm Dakota. Would you like to sample a macadamia nut white chocolate truffle?"

"No, thank you." He bit his lower lip. "I came to see Portia. Is she here?"

"No, she isn't." Not a lie. Dakota was grateful for that. She only wished she knew where Portia was.

Hurt flashed in his eyes. "Do you know when she'll be back?"

"I don't."

Which, again, was the truth, but Dakota's concern was growing by the second. She kept listening for the back door to open. It hadn't. She needed to find Portia, but first Dakota had to get rid of Austin.

She kept a smile on her face. "Would you like me to give her a message?"

"Please." The young man straightened. "Could you give her these flowers? Tell her they're from Austin and to please call me?"

His heartfelt tone sounded genuine, but then again, the guy could be a good actor. Dakota didn't know the young couple's story, but Portia's face had lost all its color. From fear or surprise? Dakota hoped the latter.

Portia might not be ready to see her ex-boyfriend or she might not be over him yet. There could be so many reasons for her reaction, including protecting her heart. But the back door hadn't opened again, which meant she still hadn't returned to the shop. That worried Dakota.

"I'm happy to give the flowers to Portia and pass on your message."

That would give Portia time to decide how she would respond to Austin Bradshaw.

"Thank you." With a forlorn look, he handed over the beautiful flowers and trudged out the door.

Dakota tried to think. She needed to find Portia, but someone from the Bar V5 would be coming to pick up their chocolate order before the shop closed at five. She glanced at the clock. That was twenty minutes away.

The bell rang. Bryce entered the shop.

Relief surged. "Thank goodness you're here."

His gaze locked on the bouquet in her hands. "Nice flowers. Decorations for the shop?"

"No." Dakota watched the cowboy head down Main Street. "They're for Portia, but she ran out of here without saying a word. She left her purse, phone, and jacket. I have no idea where she is. I'm afraid something is wrong."

"Is she in some kind of trouble?"

"I think guy trouble." Dakota didn't want to close down early and lock Portia out if she came back. "I can't leave the shop, but I need to find her. Could you please—"

"Which way did she go?" Bryce didn't hesitate.

"Out the back door. Thank you." Of course Dakota should have known he would help. Affection for him grew. Not anything new. "If you can't find Portia in the alley, you might want to check down by the river. There's a group of rocks off the path through the park where she might be."

"Why would she go there?" he asked.

"It's a good place to sit when you're mending a broken heart."

BRYCE DIDN'T SEE Portia in the alley or on any of the side streets. He quickened his pace and headed to the park.

One thought echoed through his head.

It's a good place to go when you're mending a broken heart.

He wondered if Dakota had gone there after her wedding had been canceled or if a friend had told her about the spot. He hated the idea of her being hurt by anyone.

Bryce scanned the area. No sign of Portia. He heard the sound of water flowing in the distance. Must be the Marietta River.

He came upon a paved path and followed it into the park. The water sounded louder. Faster. He must be getting close.

An outcrop of rocks was directly in front of him. A lone figure sat on them. A woman. Portia.

He breathed a sigh of relief. For all their sakes.

She wore an apron over her clothes. Her arms were crossed in front of her.

He climbed up onto the rocks and sat next to her. "I'm Bryce."

"Walt's son."

Bryce nodded. "Dakota sent me. She's worried about you."

"I'm sorry."

"We found you. That's all that matters."

"Is he gone?" Portia asked.

Bryce wasn't sure who she meant. Probably the guy who'd brought the flowers. "There was no one else in the shop besides Dakota when I arrived."

Portia exhaled. "Thank goodness."

Bryce had no idea what to say, but he knew one thing he could do. He removed his coat and covered her shoulders with it. "Someone left flowers for you."

Her gaze jerked from the river to him. "He did?"

Bryce nodded. Jealousy had hit hard and fast when he saw the bouquet in Dakota's hands. He'd been so happy to find out they weren't for her. That was the last way he expected to feel since they were…

He wasn't sure what they were.

Friends. He'd never felt like he wanted to punch another guy over a friend.

The water flowed fast. The sound soothed.

Was that why people came here?

Bryce didn't know Portia outside of visiting the chocolate shop, but he knew something was wrong. "Is there anything I can do to help?"

"Thanks, but there's nothing anyone can do."

He didn't know what to say. Maybe he didn't need to.

"Okay, but I'm a good listener if you need to talk."

Staring at the water, Portia took a breath and then another. "Have you ever wanted something so badly only to find out that it wasn't what you needed?"

An image of Chelsea Fordham popped into his mind. Funny, but he hadn't thought of her in weeks. "Yes."

"Me, too. Now I realize I made a big mistake, and there's no easy way to fix it."

Bryce wanted to help this young woman, but wasn't sure how. If only Dakota was here or… "My mom told me some of the best things in life happen because of the mistakes we make."

The corners of Portia's mouth curved upward. "That sounds like something Dakota might say."

"Yeah, it does." There were a few other ways Dakota was like his mom, but he hadn't thought of this one. "My mom also said mistakes were good because at least you were trying something new or taking a chance instead of not doing anything at all."

"I took a chance. A big one." Portia hugged herself. "Now I keep changing my mind, and it's driving me crazy."

"You might need more time to figure out exactly what you want."

"If only it were that easy, not so…"

"Impossible."

"Exactly."

"My mom also told me if something is right, you'll know

it because everything inside you feels good, but if something is wrong, you'll know that, too." He patted his chest. Funny, he'd forgotten about that until now. "Because you get this icky feeling right here. One that doesn't go away even if you try to ignore it."

Portia's eyes widened. She placed her palm over her chest. "Right here?"

"Yes. Know the feeling?"

She nodded.

Maybe she had that icky feeling right now, but he didn't want to push too hard. He needed to get her inside where she could warm up. He stood. "Let's head back to the chocolate shop. Dakota is waiting, and there's hot chocolate."

"Now *you* sound like Dakota."

"Don't let her hear you say that."

Portia hesitated. She stared at the rushing water. "What if…"

"I won't let anyone come near you, if you don't want them to. I'm happy to drive you home from the chocolate shop." He extended his arm to help her up. "Deal?"

"Deal." Portia took his hand, stood, and headed to the path.

Bryce fell in step with her. He had no idea if he'd helped Portia. He doubted it, but she would be back at the shop. That would make Dakota happy. Making her happy pleased him.

He wished he could do more for Dakota than just help walk dogs and do rescue work.

Maybe there was something—he could take her out to eat at her favorite place in town. They could go after he drove Portia home and they walked the dogs.

What was the worst thing that could happen if he asked her to dinner?

Hearing her say yes was worth the risk of hearing a no.

STREETLIGHTS ILLUMINATED THE sidewalk outside the Main Street Diner, but Dakota saw few others out and about even though it wasn't that late. She didn't mind. More time where she didn't have to share Bryce.

The chill in the air didn't bother her. She felt warm inside and not the least bit cold with Bryce next to her.

Dakota walked with a bounce to her step. She'd been working so hard, but at this moment, she felt as light as a fallen leaf about to be blown away. One person was to thank.

Bryce.

She glanced sideways at him.

Her heart thumped in her chest.

He was handsome, caring, and her date.

D-A-T-E.

They were on an official date, and she was as giddy as a teenager. Guess that was what happened after a year plus sabbatical from going out with men. Or it could be her date himself. Maybe that was why tonight was so much fun.

The entire date, so far, had been good—from his invitation back at the chocolate shop, to their conversation over the tasty meal, to the way his hand now rested at the small of her back.

Kelly had been right about not being so quick to say no. Dakota was happy she'd said yes.

"So where were we?" Bryce asked.

"It's my turn." They'd been asking each other random questions since before they'd left the restaurant. "Should Christmas carols be played before Black Friday or not?"

"That's an easy one. Not."

"I agree." One more thing they had in common.

"My turn," he said. "Coffee or tea?"

The chocolate shop was up ahead. "Hot chocolate."

"That wasn't a choice."

"I know, but that's my answer because it's what I prefer to drink."

He pointed to the shop's front door. "Because you work here."

"Yes and no. Even if I didn't work here, I'd still love chocolate and prefer hot cocoa over everything else."

"I get that."

"What don't you like about chocolate?"

His gaze lowered from hers. "Is that your question for me?"

"Yes. I'd like to know."

His hand slipped off her back. "Because you work at a chocolate shop?"

"Because I want to get to know you better."

He rubbed the back of his neck. "It's not the best story."

"I'd still like to hear it."

"Okay." Bryce shoved his hands in his pockets. "I was ten, and it was Halloween. I went trick-or-treating with a friend from the neighborhood. When we finished, Mike and I had the stupid idea to have a candy bar eating contest."

"Uh-oh."

"Exactly." Bryce shook his head. "I won, but I spent the night throwing up."

"And you haven't eaten chocolate since then."

"Would you?"

"Probably not." That had to have been awful. "But if you're ever tempted—"

"I am right now, but not for chocolate." The desire filling his gaze sent heat pouring through her veins. "I want to kiss you. I've wanted to do that for a while now."

Thank goodness. She swallowed. "I want to kiss you, too."

She wasn't sure who made the first move—him or her, but lips connected. Mouths moved over each other. Bodies pressed together.

His arms wrapped around her. Leaning closer, she raised her hands to his shoulders.

So solid and strong. An unfamiliar sense of belonging grabbed hold of her.

Kissing him now was better than the first time.

Tingles erupted and nerve endings danced.

His kiss teased and flirted, hinted at what could come.

Better than chocolate?

Oh, yeah.

She wanted to give into the pleasurable sensations pulsing through her. She wanted to lose control. She wanted…

Him.

Did she dare?

Kelly's words rushed back to Dakota.

A man doesn't have to be one or the other. He can fall in between. A Mr. Maybe or a Mr. Right Now. You'd need to keep things casual since you know there's an end date.

Being with Bryce didn't feel casual. Neither did his kiss.

But that didn't change the fact there was an end date in sight. He would return to Seattle soon.

His hands wove through her hair, and his mouth showered more kisses.

So good.

But was she setting herself up for disappointment and heartache if she spent more time with Bryce? Kept kissing him like this? Or when the time came for him to return to Seattle, could she say goodbye without any regrets? With a happy heart?

She didn't know.

That bothered her.

And scared her.

But excited her, too.

Chapter Twelve

OVER THE NEXT week, Bryce fell into a comfortable pattern, one that made him happy and content to be in Marietta for a little while longer. He spent his days with his father and also worked on his proposal. That was coming together, and his assistant was putting the final touches on what he'd submit when he returned home.

The late afternoon and evenings belonged to Dakota. The two of them would walk the dogs, but since their dinner out, they hadn't said goodbye after the walks. They'd done something together—grabbed a bite to eat, watched a movie, or worked on rescue stuff. Things were casual, and he liked that.

He hadn't been looking for someone to date, but spending time with Dakota made him feel good about himself, about life. He understood why his father had been pushing them together. She was different from other women he'd dated. Dakota was…special. If she lived in Seattle, he could see them becoming a couple.

But she didn't, and he did.

Dating while he was in Marietta was all this could be, and that was okay. But tonight, standing in Copper Mountain Chocolates with over a dozen others, he felt more like a full-fledged boyfriend, not a date.

Attending this event went beyond everything he'd done since he arrived in Marietta. Although he had to admit Dakota looked adorable in the pilgrim hat and white collar she wore over her black dress. The three other women who worked at the shop—Sage, Portia, and Rosie—were dressed the same.

Soft instrumental music played. Other participants chatted. Some of the people he recognized from around town and the adoption events. Others he didn't know, but everyone was friendly.

Bryce wore a copper-colored apron and stood in front of pieces of chocolate he was supposed to put together somehow. Okay, tonight wasn't his worst nightmare since clowns weren't involved, but this was a close second with chocolate involved.

He sighed. "I can't believe I'm doing this."

Dakota patted his hand. "Walt wanted to come, but there isn't room for his wheelchair. You're doing this for him."

That didn't make Bryce feel better. "What are we making?"

"A chocolate cornucopia filled with all kinds of yummies you won't eat." She leaned closer and whispered, "But don't forget, there's pie."

"The one saving grace." Although, he hoped to be rewarded for being a good sport with a kiss later.

"Welcome to Copper Mountain Chocolates," Sage said to the guests. "We're so excited to have you here tonight. Chocolates aren't something you might normally associate with Thanksgiving, but we've come up with a fun treat you can make to keep for yourself or give as a hostess gift. We even have ribbon and decorations you can add to the box containing your finished product."

Crafting? Just shoot him now. He was a guy. Guys didn't craft.

A six-pack of beer worked just fine as a gift if he was going over to someone's house. "Dad is going to owe me big time."

Dakota kissed his cheek. "You'll survive. You might even have fun."

"You're going to owe me, too." He raised an eyebrow.

A blush tinged her cheeks. She handed him a pair of disposable gloves. "I'm sure we can figure out a way to repay you."

Now that might turn this cornucopia making into something worthwhile.

That, and, he smiled, the pie.

THE DAYS FLEW by. Dakota cleaned the four tables at the

chocolate shop. A smile had been on her face for the past week and showed no signs of going away.

The reason—Bryce.

Granted, more animals were being adopted, including the two rabbits who'd arrived the day the pipe broke, and she'd heard nothing but compliments about the *Make Your Own Chocolate Thanksgiving Cornucopia and Pie* event.

But holding hands while walking dogs and spending time together made the sun shine brighter, the color of the changing leaves a deeper hue, and the world feel like a better place.

Silly, yes, and she didn't mind one bit.

He'd told her about wanting Walt to move to Seattle, and she'd decided not to get involved in that discussion. The father and son needed to decide that one without her input.

Something clattered against the floor near the cash register where Portia was working.

Dakota dropped her rag on a table to see what had happened.

Portia clutched the countertop behind the glass display case. The blood had completely drained from her face. She not only looked pale, but also a little green. The tray of samples and silver tongs lay on the floor.

Dakota ran and put her arm around Portia's waist. "You're so pale."

"I'm tired. That's all."

The way she hadn't let go of the counter suggested otherwise.

Concerned, Dakota led Portia to a chair. "Sit."

"I'm—"

"You need to rest."

Portia sat.

Dakota's concern rose. "You haven't been feeling well for a couple of weeks now. Have you been to a doctor?"

"Yes." Portia stared at the floor. "I wanted to tell you, but I…I was too nervous."

"Tell me what?"

"I-I'm pregnant."

Dakota let the words sink in. The physical signs had been there—fatigue, nausea, feeling faint—as well as Portia wanting to work more to save money, but this wasn't what Dakota had expected to hear from the slim young woman. However, her surprise was nothing compared to what Portia was facing. "How far along are you?"

"Three months."

That explained why Portia wasn't showing yet.

"Stay here," Dakota said. "I'll be right back."

She moistened a towel and filled a glass with water. She wondered if the pregnancy had anything to do with the way Portia bolted when Austin showed up, but that was no one's business but Portia's.

"Take a few sips slowly." Dakota handed Portia the glass and then blotted her forehead. "If Sage was here, she'd do the same thing."

"Or send me home."

Portia's need for breaks right away made sense now. "Yes, so be glad it's just you and me here."

Portia's shoulders drooped. Her eyelids looked heavy.

"You need a nap. I'll help you to the back where you can rest."

"I'm pregnant, not an invalid."

"You look too tired to walk."

"I haven't been sleeping well."

"I'll clean up." Dakota would do the tasks on the closing checklist, so Portia could rest. "I have no idea what you're going through, but I want you to know I'm here for you. Whatever you need. Whenever you need it. No questions asked."

Portia's eyes gleamed. "Thanks. It's been…overwhelming."

Dakota hugged her. "Does your mother know?"

"No, just Aunt Sage and Rosie. And now you."

"Your secret is safe."

"I know." Portia exhaled loudly. "I'm scared."

"I would be, too."

Portia laughed.

"What I mean is I think however you're feeling—scared, happy, nervous, excited, overwhelmed—is normal. And I know what you need besides a nap."

Portia yawned. "What?"

Dakota smiled. "Another hug and as soon as you are

rested, a mug of hot chocolate."

STARING AT THE calendar in the kitchen, Bryce couldn't believe today was Monday and there were only three more days until Thanksgiving. Three more days to polish his proposal. Three more days to spend with Dakota. Three more days to convince his dad to move.

That was enough time, wasn't it?

Bryce didn't leave for Seattle until Saturday, but he wanted to spend his final days here packing his dad's stuff. He had estimates from moving companies and a tentative plan in his head. Now all he needed was for his dad to go along.

He poured two cups of coffee, added a dash of cream and a teaspoon of sugar to his dad's, and carried the steaming mugs to the living room. He placed the cup on the end table next to his dad's recliner and then took a seat on the couch.

His father took a sip. "Are you seeing Dakota tonight?"

"She's going to stop by after a meeting at the rescue."

"She's getting those animals adopted." His father sounded proud.

"Yes."

But Bryce didn't like how tired Dakota looked, and she seemed even more worried about Portia for some reason. Today was one of her days off from the chocolate shop, but she hadn't slept in based on the time of her first text this morning. That worried him. Each day he spent with Dakota, he found himself caring more about her. He wanted to be able to have more input into what she did and didn't do. He wanted more time with her. Not what he expected to have happened, and if he didn't know better, he'd think he was falling for her, but things would return to normal once he was back in Seattle.

"But she's not sleeping much as a result," he added.

"Sleep is overrated when you're trying to make your dream a reality."

"Says the man who takes three naps a day."

"Dakota can rest after Thanksgiving. Just like I'm catching up on my sleep after spending most of my life working. Wait until these casts are off. I'll be ready to go."

This was the opening Bryce needed. "Then what?"

"My life will get back to normal—work and volunteering."

"You'll be lonely."

His father's gray brows drew together, and he made a funny face. "Where did you get the idea I'm lonely?"

"Volunteering, playing cards, being a regular at the chocolate shop. Look at all you've been doing."

"Those things don't mean I'm lonely. It means I'm part of a community and have a life. Friends."

"Your friends are coming over because you broke your legs."

"I saw my friends as much when my legs weren't broken,

only we didn't always meet at my house and never during the day unless it was a weekend. They come here now because it's more convenient for you and me."

Bryce tried to figure out if his father was being honest or stretching the truth. "Seriously?"

His dad nodded. "In case you haven't noticed, I have more friends in Marietta than your mother and I had in Philadelphia, and we lived there longer."

"If that's the case, you'll be able to make new friends in Seattle."

"I like the ones I have."

His father needed to be reasonable. "Marietta is too far away. We need to live closer. I've enjoyed hanging out with you this month. I realize how much time we've missed together and how much I appreciate you. That's why Seattle is the best choice.

"For you, not for me."

"You're my last living relative. Family. I'm right about this, Dad."

"You're wrong, son." His father's jaw tensed. "Your mother's dream brought me here, and I'm so happy I listened to her. You are family, but Marietta is my home. I'm not moving."

"But—"

"Nothing you say is going to change my mind." His gaze hardened like granite. "In case you've forgotten, I buried your mother's ashes here in Marietta, and there's a spot waiting next to her for me. Nothing, not even you, is going to take me away from this town, so please stop trying. It's only going to drive a wedge between us, and that's the last thing I want when you'll be leaving in a few days."

Hurt sliced through Bryce. Jagged. Raw.

The air seemed to disappear from his lungs, and he had to force himself to breathe. All he could think about was how he hadn't been there for his mom. He'd wanted to be a good son, but he'd failed in the worst way. He couldn't let that happen again with his dad. "What if something happens to you?"

"You're my emergency contact."

"Dad—"

"If something happens again, you'll do what you did this time. You call the airlines and get here as soon as you can."

But what if he couldn't get here in time? What if his dad ended up like his mom?

No, he would miss his father too much if they weren't together. Bryce wasn't giving up. Somehow, he would convince his father to move with him. He still had time.

AFTER THE MEETING with the adoption committee, Dakota drove to Walt's house. She couldn't wait to update Bryce on the new number of adoptions. Almost giddy, she knocked three times.

He opened the door. "How many?"

"Fifty-four. Can you believe it?" She raised a pie box from the Copper Mountain Gingerbread and Dessert Factory. "I brought pie to celebrate, but first I want a kiss."

He obliged with a brush of his lips.

More like a peck. Not how he normally kissed her.

Maybe he was hungry for pie.

"My dad went to bed early. We argued about his moving to Seattle." Bryce closed the door. "Let's go into the kitchen, so we don't disturb him."

She followed Bryce and sat across from him at the table. Now that there was more light, she noticed lines around his mouth and on his forehead. His face looked tighter, as if he were upset. "Are you doing okay?"

"I'm better now that you're here."

His words made her happy. That was how seeing him made her feel, but she wished he would drop this plan to move Walt to Seattle. Obviously, his father didn't want to go.

Bryce sliced and served the pie. "How did you know I loved apple?"

"It's my favorite, and there's no chocolate."

"A win for both of us." He took a bite and flashed the thumbs-up sign. "Do you have plans for Thanksgiving?"

That got her attention. She straightened.

"I've been so busy I haven't made plans yet." Dakota would love nothing more than to spend the holiday with him and Walt. "How about you?"

"My dad and I are going to eat dinner at the Graff."

That sounded definite, as if reservations had been made. A party of two, not three.

A bolt of disappointment streaked across her chest.

Ignore it.

She shouldn't be upset. They hadn't known each other long. They'd been acting like a couple for an even shorter time. Spending the holiday together had never been a given or assumed.

"You and your dad will be having a fancy turkey dinner." She forced a smile. This didn't matter.

Bryce would soon be back in Seattle, a world away from Marietta. The realization hurt more than she thought it should since she'd gone into this with her eyes wide open.

Casual, fun, known end date.

"I've heard the dinners are amazing." She'd eaten lunch there and been to the bar for happy hour with Kelly. Each December, Dakota also paid a visit to see Santa and to view the gingerbread houses on display during the Marietta stroll.

"That's what I've been told." Bryce scooped up another forkful of pie. "The Graff was my dad's idea. He didn't want any of his lady friends to feel obligated to cook dinner for us."

"That's thoughtful, though I doubt any of his lady friends would mind." She would have gladly cooked for the two Grayson men, but she'd been too busy to think about the holiday yet.

"My father is thoughtful to everyone except his own son." Frustration laced Bryce's words. The corners of his mouth turned downward. "I don't know what to say that'll make him see that moving to Seattle is the right choice."

"That's your father's decision, not yours."

Bryce pushed his plate toward the center of the kitchen table. "I'm going to keep trying, even if it ruins Thanksgiving dinner."

None of her business. She'd planned to stay out of it, but she cared about Bryce and Walt. She didn't want their holiday ruined over this.

"Please don't. Not saying anything for one day won't matter," she urged. "The word 'thanks' is part of Thanksgiving for a reason. It's a day to be thankful, not to argue."

"I'll be thankful when my dad is in Seattle and far away from this place."

His harsh tone suggested he hated Marietta. That must be emotion talking, not him, right?

She set her fork on the plate. "There must be a few other things you're thankful for."

"Such as?"

"I'm thankful for my family, friends, jobs, house, animals, and chocolate."

And Bryce. But she wasn't ready to say his name aloud in front of him.

"You can rattle off a list because you have a thankful heart," he said. "All of those things mean something to you."

They did. Especially him.

Oh, no.

Another bolt zigzagged across her chest. Not disappointment.

Love.

She felt as if a frozen turkey had been dropped on her head.

She was falling for Bryce. Falling hard.

Dakota swallowed. "What things would be on your list?"

Me.

She desperately wanted him to say her.

"I know one," Bryce said. "I'm thankful for my dad."

"That's good. Anything else?" She forced the words out her dry throat. "Special times? Or a special person?"

"Not really."

His words stabbed her heart like a dagger. "Are you sure?"

He nodded.

Neither she nor the time they'd spent together meant anything to him. Her shoulders sagged.

"I do know something I could be thankful for," he said finally.

She perked up. "What?"

"I'd be very thankful if my dad knew what was good for him."

Not what she wanted to hear. Maybe she was reading too much into this. Bryce was upset at his father. That could color what he was thinking and saying. He was being irrational and stubborn about wanting to move his father.

"I know you want your dad in Seattle, but maybe Walt does know what's good for him," she said.

Bryce's gaze jerked up from the pie to her. "What do you mean?"

"Walt's created a life for himself in Marietta. The location may be inconvenient to you, but it works for him."

Dakota needed to say this for Walt's sake and Bryce's, too.

"What is this move really about?" she asked. "You or your father?"

"My dad." The words tumbled out.

"Sure about that?"

"Yes." Bryce sounded adamant.

"Then shouldn't your dad's happiness be the most important thing?"

"It is. He lives alone."

"Your father lives alone, but so do I and lots of other people. You live alone in Seattle."

"That's different."

"Why?"

"It's me. My father needs help."

"Someday, Walt might need around-the-clock care and assistance now, but once his legs heal, he'll be fine on his own."

"If something happens—"

"He's surrounded by people who care about him," she interrupted. "Yes, you're his son, but others like me can hold down the fort until you arrive. Just like we did a few weeks ago."

Bryce hesitated. "So I should go home. By myself."

"Unless you want to stick around Marietta longer."

There. She'd said it.

Dakota held her breath.

He flinched. "Why would I want to stay here?"

Sharp claws pierced her heart way deeper than the dagger had gone. Guess he had managed to keep any feelings for her from developing. That was what she'd hoped to do, but still…

She raised her chin and released the breath she'd been holding. "To spend more time with your dad."

"I suppose I could come back at Christmastime."

Okay, maybe she hadn't fallen for the wrong guy again. She crossed her fingers. "That would be wonderful."

Bryce nodded. "It would give me more time to talk my father into moving to Seattle."

Unbelievable. Bryce acted like a nice guy. He'd done nice guy things for the past three weeks. But he wasn't nice. He was selfish. And arrogant. He wanted what he thought was best, not what might be best for his father.

Frustration prickled. "Have you not heard a word I said?"

"Yes, but…" Bryce leaned over the table. His eyes lit up.

"You can help me."

"How?"

"Convince my father that Seattle is the best place for him. You're his friend. He'll listen to you."

She scooted back in the chair. "No."

"Why not?"

She might as well say it. "Because I don't think Seattle is the best place for him."

Or for you.

"I thought you were on my side."

"Why does there have to be sides? We both want your dad to be happy."

"Or do you not want to lose your free handyman at the rescue?"

His words hit her like a slap to the face. She flinched. "Is that what you think?"

"Why else would you want my dad to stay here?"

Her heart splintered. Her breath hitched. She touched her chest. It didn't stop the pain from spreading through her.

Stay calm.

She knew he said things when emotion got the best of him. He'd done it twice before with her. Could that be why he was doing this now?

"Is that what you think about me?" Her eyes implored Bryce. "Really?"

He said nothing. But he didn't need to speak, his facial expression said enough.

Dakota wanted to make him understand that he was wrong. She opened her mouth to state her case, but pressed her lips together instead. She shouldn't have to defend herself.

If he knew her the way she thought he did, he would have never said those words. And if he cared about her, even a little bit, he would be apologizing.

But he didn't.

Hadn't.

Wouldn't.

"Well, then." She stood. "There's nothing left to say except goodbye."

With as much dignity as she could muster, she walked out of the kitchen, through the living room, and out the front door. The temptation to glance over her shoulder was strong, but she didn't dare.

Nothing she said or did would make a difference.

Not with Bryce.

Her tight chest made breathing difficult. A lump burned in her throat. Tears stung her eyes, but she wouldn't cry. She'd shed too many tears the last time she'd had her heart broken.

Dakota had only herself to blame. She'd let herself fall for him, even though she'd known better. In spite of wanting to be smarter this time, she couldn't control her feelings and emotions. Once again, she'd fallen into the same trap and repeated the same pattern by going out with another Mr.

Wrong.

All because she'd wanted...love.

That mythical four-letter word.

She would have been better off sticking to chocolate and her foster animals.

What a fool she'd been for thinking they shared something special. Thinking he knew her. Thinking he cared.

Bryce hadn't.

Everything had been in her mind, fueled by a romantic imagination and a longing for a happily ever after. When would she learn unicorns didn't exist and rainbows were a scientific phenomenon? Nothing more.

She didn't feel in control enough to drive, so she walked past her car and quickened her pace to get home faster.

Face it. She'd been nothing to him other than someone to pass the time with while he was in Marietta—a place where he knew no one but his father. What they'd shared—the time together and the hot kisses—hadn't been special or meaningful.

And that meant she hadn't been that to him, either.

Tears burned. She blinked them away, and then ran.

Dakota didn't care who saw her. She needed to get home now. Before she lost it.

Big time.

GOODBYE.

Bryce stood on his father's front porch. The cold night

air surrounded him and gave him goose bumps, but he didn't move. He kept waiting for Dakota to come back, to call him out on what he'd said, but she hadn't and likely wouldn't.

Is that what you really think about me?

The hurt in her eyes had matched the anguish in her voice.

He'd said the words in the heat of the moment, but apologizing had never crossed his mind.

Because in the midst of arguing with Dakota, he'd realized this was happening for a reason—so he could distance himself from her. He hadn't done that on purpose, but now he didn't have to worry about leaving her after Thanksgiving. Sure, he felt like a bigger jerk than he had the two times he'd said the wrong thing to her. But this time, his mistake was a good one.

Dakota would thank him for this.

Not today, tomorrow, or next week. But someday.

She might look like an angel, but she was more like a devil tempting him with her sweet kisses and making him want more. He wasn't in a position for more.

Not when he was going back to Seattle.

Saying goodbye was for the best.

For him.

For her.

A little hurt now was better than a lot of hurt later.

And that was where this was headed if they continued

seeing each other through Thanksgiving.

Now they would avoid an awkward, painful goodbye when it came time for him to leave.

No wondering what might have been or futile attempts at dating long distance.

Yes, breaking up now was for the best. And not just to make their goodbye easier.

What she'd said about his father pissed Bryce off.

No one knew what was better for Walt Grayson than his own son. Dakota should want to help, not stand in Bryce's way of getting what he wanted.

Scratch that—what he *needed* to happen.

He walked inside and closed the door.

For the best.

He repeated the words.

Now she wouldn't miss him after he left. He would be able to stop caring and wanting more with her. He could focus on his father. That had been the original plan anyway.

But that didn't stop a weight from pressing down on Bryce as if he were carrying bags of cement powder on each shoulder.

But maybe he would feel better in the morning.

Things could look better in the daylight.

Dakota had said that the day they met. She'd been correct then. He hoped she was right this time, too.

NOT EVEN CHOCOLATE helped Dakota feel better. Nothing

did.

She filled a box of assorted chocolates using silver tongs. Her smile was forced, but she didn't have a choice. Sage expected the staff to provide customer service with a smile.

"Have more animals found homes?" Rachel Vaughn picked up a toy her baby daughter had dropped from the stroller. Rachel not only owned the bakery in town, but she was also married to one of the co-owners of the Bar V5 Dude Ranch. Her brother, Ty Murphy, was the other owner.

"We're close." Dakota tied the box with ribbon. "Two more who were at a rescue in Bozeman were adopted yesterday."

"You'll do it."

"Thanks. We have a couple of days left."

She'd accomplished more adoptions this month than anyone at the rescue thought she'd do, including Lori. The donation still wasn't theirs, but everyone was hopeful they'd get it.

But Dakota worried about Rascal. He needed more training or someone who would invest the time and money into obedience lessons.

She placed the box of candy in a bag and handed it to Rachel. "Have a great day."

Her voice almost sounded cheery. Progress?

"Thanks." Rachel pushed the stroller out of the store.

Sage came out of the back. The copper apron brought out the natural color in her face and made her hair look fiery.

"Portia called me. She's not feeling well. I'm going to cover the rest of her shift."

Thinking about the Portia's situation put Dakota's into perspective. Things could be much worse for her. "They shouldn't call it morning sickness when it lasts all day."

Surprise filled Sage's expression. "So you know? Portia told you?"

Dakota nodded. "Her ex Austin came by the shop looking for her."

"I wish I knew what was going on."

"That's as much as I know. Portia will tell us when she's ready."

"I hope so." Sage rearranged the tongs. "How are you doing?"

"I'm good."

"I haven't seen Bryce around."

Dakota shrugged. "Me, either."

Sage's brows drew together. "You're okay with that?"

Was she? "He's going back to Seattle. This was doomed from the start."

She'd known that logically at the beginning, but his toe-curling kisses and attention had blinded her to the truth. She'd only seen the parts of him that she wanted to see. She still had no idea how to choose a man because Bryce was another Mr. Wrong.

"But maybe there's some other guy out there who wants to stick around Marietta. And likes dogs and chocolates as much as I do."

Sage smile softly. "I'm sure there is."

"I'm going to clean." Dakota put on gloves and grabbed a rag from the bleach to wipe down the tables.

"I'll straighten back here."

Of course, Dakota had already done that. Sage, however, had exacting standards. That was what made their boss and her chocolates so special.

Dakota stepped around the counter.

"Just remember," Sage said. "Love seems to find you when you're not looking for it. That's what happened to me."

"I'll remember that. Thanks."

Love had found Kelly at Grey's Saloon with that cowboy who'd asked her out. The two had been dating ever since. Dakota was happy for her best friend, but she wasn't going to find love when her heart needed time to heal.

Until then, she would take care of her foster animals and indulge in chocolate. Not a bad way to bide her time, but after Bryce, she'd learned she needed more balance in her life. Volunteering filled her heart with joy and the animals gave her the love she so craved, but she'd gone overboard, especially after Craig. Never taking a day off for herself was stupid. She could volunteer, but still have fun and do things for herself, too.

And speaking of Craig and Bryce and all the other Mr. Wrongs in her past...

It was time to shut down the Chocolate Is Better Than Men Club. The CIBTMC had begun as a joke between her and Kelly, and as the only remaining member, Dakota knew the time had come to disband. She needed to look forward, not back.

And she would.

Starting this weekend, she would work on her house. She'd talked about putting down roots, and she'd lived longer in Marietta than she had anywhere else, but she'd yet to make the house her own. No more putting off the projects she wanted to do until York or Nevada was around. Three years was too long to feel like a guest in your own home. It was time to change that.

No more imagining what the house could look like someday. Dakota had her inheritance.

Time to turn her dreams into reality.

Chapter Thirteen

DAKOTA DIDN'T KNOW why Walt had invited her over. She hoped he wasn't trying to get her and Bryce back together. Not that they'd been dating long. If what they had done could even be called dating. But this was Walt, and she wasn't going to avoid him, so after work, she headed over to his house.

Standing on his front porch, she blew out a puff of air and rang the doorbell.

"It's open," Walt called. "Come in."

Pasting on a smile, she stepped through the door and held up the Copper Mountain Chocolates bag. "I brought chocolate."

"You're the best."

If only Bryce thought so. No. Don't think about him.

She crossed the living room and handed Walt the small bag. "Sage made her dark chocolate cherry hazelnut bark this morning."

Walt took a peek inside. "Yum."

Dakota wiped her sweaty palms on the thighs of her

jeans. "So what's up?"

Please don't let it be Bryce.

"I want to adopt Scout and Pierre."

A mix of emotion flashed through her—surprise, regret, relief, and pure joy. A Mastiff seemed to be pressing against her chest. She struggled for a breath. "Really?"

"Yes." The smile on his face confirmed the words. "The two are a bonded pair, and they would do better if they stayed together."

"They would, but are you up for handling two pets?"

"Pierre is easy since he doesn't go outside. I can have Bryce install a doggy door for Scout, and once I'm back on my feet, I'll be able to take him for walks."

She ignored the pang hearing Bryce's name brought. "You've thought about this."

"I've been thinking about it for a while now," Walt admitted. "It might not be the perfect time with my legs, but a home needs animals, and those two are right for me."

Dakota grinned. "I'm convinced."

Her heart filled with affection for this man who'd done so much for the rescue. Two more names could be crossed off her list. Maybe they would make the Thanksgiving deadline.

"Scout and Pierre are so lucky," she said. "They will have a wonderful home with you."

"I'm the lucky one."

One question hammered at her brain. Dakota needed to

ask it, even if she wasn't sure she wanted to hear the answer. "Have you spoken to Bryce about this?"

"No. He can't see past getting me to move to Seattle, but he'll come around to my staying in Marietta and adopting the two."

Her shoulders sagged. "Walt—"

"My son is only thinking about what he wants. I'm not moving to Seattle. This is my home, and I intend to stay here with Scout and Pierre."

The certainty in Walt's voice didn't ease her concerns. His decision wasn't going to sit well with Bryce, but she couldn't do anything about that. Bryce didn't want to listen to reason. Not from his father and not from her.

"I understand." But that didn't lessen her worry for the two men. "I hope this adoption doesn't drive you and your son farther apart."

"My son may have shown up in Marietta because of my broken legs, but he arrived with an ulterior motive. This is the first time he's visited since I moved here three years ago. From the get-go, all he could talk about is how great Seattle is versus how little Marietta has to offer. I may be old, but I'm not going to be talked into doing something that will make me unhappy because my son feels bad for not coming home all those times his mother asked. We'll get through this once Bryce realizes he's being driven by guilt, nothing more."

"You have it all figured out."

"I know Bryce. He's more like his mother, but I can see a lot of myself in him."

She saw similarities between the two Graysons. Each wanted the other to move. That was why Walt had played matchmaker. Both men had failed. But the differences between the two were more striking. Walt was about community and service, whereas Bryce focused on himself and his needs.

Maybe someday, she'd come to realize that things had worked out for the best. She'd finally realized that with Craig, but the pain she felt now over Bryce was so raw. It was too soon to rationalize anything. Her heart hurt too much.

"How soon before Scout and Pierre can move in?" Walt asked.

"I'll turn in the paperwork tonight. Since you're a long-time volunteer, the approval process is a formality. I can bring them over tonight, unless you'd rather wait until the morning. I could come before my shift."

"Tomorrow. You and Rascal can have one more night with them." Walt rubbed his hands together. "There's so much I'm going to need."

"I can help with that."

"I was hoping you'd offer."

Walt's excitement warmed her heart. She hoped Bryce would be happy for his father. "You can use Pierre's current cage until I can get you a new one."

"Thank you. I'm also drawing up plans to construct a rat habitat. Would you like to see?"

Anticipation filled Walt's voice. He sounded more like a ten-year-old boy than a grown man.

A much-needed smile spread across her face. "I'd love to see your plans for Pierre's enclosure."

AS BRYCE ENTERED the kitchen from the backyard, he heard voices in the living room. His father's and a female one.

Not one of his card-playing friends.

Dakota.

Bryce's heart beat triple time. What was she doing here?

She was friends with his dad, but he hadn't expected to find her here today. Not after last night.

This must be his father's doing.

Bryce stepped into the living room. "Hello."

Dakota sat on the couch. She held a drawing.

Uncertainty flashed in her eyes. "Hey."

"What's going on?" he asked.

"I'm showing Dakota my plans for the enclosure I'm going to build Pierre," his father answered.

Bryce's neck stiffened. "Tell me you're not going to let my dad adopt two animals."

Her smile disappeared. "Why would I stand in his way?"

"Because he doesn't need them. The only reason he wants the animals is because he's lonely. If he'd stop being so stubborn and move to Seattle, he wouldn't need to adopt and waste his time and money on pets he doesn't need."

Walt shook his head. "Bryce—"

"Pets are not a waste of time or money." Dakota stood. Her eyes darkened, and lines formed around her mouth. "Pets not only provide companionship, but they also help with their owner's stress levels and health. They are a blessing."

Figures she'd given his father the spiel that she wouldn't give to him. "You have to say that. It's your job."

"Your job as his son is to love your father and respect his decisions. Maybe you should start doing that instead of trying to make him to do something he doesn't want." She took a breath. "Just because you prefer living in a city doesn't mean it's for everyone. Instead of trying to force the issue, why not do what's best for your father? Not make him start over in a new place where he has no friends or connections except for you."

Bryce pressed his lips together. "You don't understand."

"Don't I?" She stared at him. "My parents decided to follow their dream of sailing off into the sunset, far away from their three kids. I wish they were closer, so I could see them more often, but my siblings and I never tried to talk them out of it. Not once. We supported them, helped them downsize, and moved them onto the sailboat. That's what family does for each other."

He started to speak, but then stopped himself.

Dakota folded up the plans and placed them on the coffee table. She didn't look at him, but focused her attention on his father. "Text me your shopping list, and I'll pick up what I can tonight."

She was leaving again.

Say something.

An internal voice told him to speak up.

To acknowledge her.

To apologize.

To tell her that even though he'd tried not to fall for her, he had.

But he couldn't.

"Sounds good," his father said. "If Bryce won't install the doggy door, I'll have one of my crew do it."

"That'll work." Dakota left without looking back.

His dad shook his head. "You're going to let her go?"

"What choice do I have?"

"That's what you need to figure out."

"I'm not the villain here."

His father sighed. "Could have fooled me with the way you spoke to her."

"My life is in Seattle. That's why I want you to move. We need to live closer to each other, Dad."

"Then you move here."

Bryce swore. That wasn't the reply he wanted. His stomach hardened into a stone. His head hurt so badly the pain radiated to his jaw. It wasn't supposed to be like this. "You can't expect me to uproot my entire life, leave everything behind, and move here."

"Then why would you expect me to do the same?"

Bryce started to speak and then stopped. He didn't know the answer to that question.

"That's how I feel about my life here," his dad continued. "Yet you're asking me to do just that."

Dakota's words echoed through Bryce's head.

Walt's created a life for himself in Marietta. The location may be inconvenient to you, but it works for him.

Then shouldn't your dad's happiness be the most important thing?

Yes. Bryce collapsed on the couch.

Dakota was right. She had been right all along. He'd been thinking about what he wanted, not what was best for his dad, so Bryce wouldn't repeat his past mistakes.

She'd tried to tell him, but he hadn't listened to her or to his dad. "I'm as stubborn as you are."

"So what are you going to do about it?" his father asked with a serious tone that matched his facial expression.

Bryce had no idea. He'd hurt Dakota again. Done the same thing he'd done two times earlier, only this time was worse. He'd hurt her badly. Betrayed her trust. No way would she forgive him again, and he didn't blame her for that.

He paced the length of the living room. "A simply apology isn't going to cut it."

His father rubbed his chin. "Nate Vaughn at the Bar V5

Dude Ranch always says to go big or go home."

"What if I don't want to go home?" Bryce thought about the words he'd just said and repeated them in his mind. He'd considered Seattle to be home for so long, but now...

His dad's eyes gleamed with understanding. "Then that might be your answer."

Bryce froze. Could it be that simple?

WEDNESDAY MORNING, TWO hours before her shift began at the chocolate shop, Dakota arrived to drop off Scout and Pierre. She didn't see the van in Walt's driveway. That meant Bryce wasn't here. A mix of relief and regret battled inside her.

She let the relief win.

After she unloaded supplies and the cage, she returned to the car. Rascal was in a crate in the back. "This is going to be great for Scout and Pierre, but I hope you aren't too lonely being the only animal at home."

Rascal's tail wagged.

Such a happy guy. "Let's go turn in the adoption paperwork."

Dakota drove to the rescue. Rascal would be fine in his crate at home, but she would keep him with her as long as possible this morning. He was used to seeing others during the day, so this would be a transition period for him.

Her, too.

A few minutes later, she sat in the recently repaired office. The smell of fresh paint was still in the air, and the new tile floor gleamed.

Slowly, and carefully, she typed in the information from Walt's adoption form. Two other adoption forms were waiting to be put into the database. The final two cats had found a forever home together in Livingston.

That only left Rascal from the list of adoptable pets. The remaining Lonely Hearts animals had also been placed.

"Oh, my sweet boy." She rubbed his head. "Maybe I should just keep you for myself."

His tongue hung from his mouth, as wild looking as his long fur.

Dakota could adopt him. He liked having other animals around and wouldn't cause trouble with the other animals she fostered. Except…

She'd always seen Rascal as a family dog. He loved running and playing with Bryce, and the dog was so gentle around Sage's stepdaughter Savannah and her son Braden.

Was Dakota being selfish considering this? Thinking about what was best for her and the rescue, not Rascal?

She wished she knew.

"What do you want?" Dakota asked him. "Would life with me be too boring for you?"

Rascal stared up at her with his big brown eyes full of love and adoration.

"You're not answering, but I know that look." She

reached into the desk and pulled out a treat from the stash hidden there. "Sit."

He did and then immediately stood on all fours.

"Sit," she repeated.

Once again, he did. This time, he didn't get up.

"Good boy." She gave him the dog biscuit.

"Rascal's come a long way from the wild puppy that was dropped off months ago." Lori stood in the doorway. She wore her typical outfit—a pair of jeans and a sweatshirt with a picture of an animal. Today it was a wolf. "You've done a good job with him."

"Thanks. He's been the most challenging." Dakota knocked on her desk. "So far."

"We've had an out-of-state application put in to adopt him."

The words sank in. A familiar ache grabbed hold of her already-bruised heart. "I wasn't expecting to hear that."

"Surprised me, too," Lori admitted. "According to the adopter's application, there's a secure, fenced yard and other pets in the household, who get along with animals."

Rascal wouldn't be lonely. He much preferred being with others.

Dakota's heart pounded like a bass drum. She should be ecstatic about Rascal finding a home, but a part of her was so sad at the thought of her handsome, silly boy going away.

Ridiculous.

Getting Rascal adopted was the goal. Nothing else.

He wasn't here to make her feel better. He deserved a family of his own. "Any kids?"

"Not yet."

That meant there could be someday. "If Rascal is adopted…"

"We reach our goal." Lori finished the sentence for her. "But we aren't loosening our adoption criteria to get the donation. This has to be the right fit for Rascal and the adopter."

"I agree, especially since he needs more obedience training." Dakota bit her lip. "Is it a good fit?"

"Yes. I believe it's a perfect fit for him."

Air didn't want to go into her lungs. She forced herself to take a deep breath.

Lori's gaze traveled from Rascal to Dakota. "I'm sorry for not supporting your original *Home for the Holidays* proposal. You weren't being too optimistic. I see now you had a plan to implement—all the steps just weren't on the page."

"I was told less isn't always better."

Lori nodded. "After being in animal rescue for so long, it's easy to see everything that's wrong with the system and be blinded to the possibilities of what could turn out right."

"I understand." Dakota couldn't imagine what Lori dealt with as the director. She had to oversee everything—animals, facility, staff, volunteers, and a budget. "You have a difficult job."

"We all do here, including volunteers like you. I know

the time you put into each animal that comes through the doors." Lori's gaze softened. "Thank you."

The director didn't offer praise often, and this was more than Dakota had ever expected. "So do you have any idea who the mysterious benefactor is?"

"No, but his lawyer has an office in Bozeman."

"That doesn't tell us much."

"No."

Maybe the person would come forward when they presented the donation. Dakota stared at the dog. "So about Rascal? How will we approve his out-of-state adopter?"

"This is a personal acquaintance. I'll handle the details since you have to work at the chocolate shop today."

"Thanks." She placed her hand on Rascal, who leaned against her leg. He was such a sweetie. "When will he go to his new home?"

"Tonight."

Her mouth gaped. "That soon?"

"Tomorrow's Thanksgiving. The adopter will be having dinner with family, but I don't want you to have to come in on a holiday."

Not that Dakota had any plans. She'd spend turkey day alone. She'd turned down three dinner invites. She didn't want to be a downer on the holiday.

And now she'd be missing Rascal, too. The way he lumbered through the house and knocked things over when he bumped into the coffee table or nightstand. The way he exuberantly welcomed her home whether she was coming from the chocolate shop or the mailbox out front.

"Should I leave him here today?"

"Take him home," Lori said. "Come back with him after you get off work. You can meet his adopter."

"Sounds great." Dakota tried to muster her excitement. She tamped down the urge to submit her own application for the puppy. "There are a few things I want them to know about Rascal. I can add notes to his folder, too."

"Whatever you think is best."

Dakota wasn't sure what was best right now. She kept her hand on Rascal. "We did it."

"We did. Thanks to your hard work." Lori grinned. "Congratulations."

So why didn't Dakota feel happier? Or want to celebrate?

She hugged Rascal and didn't want to let go.

AFTER WORK, DAKOTA ignored her heavy heart and brought Rascal back to the rescue. She'd packed his food, treats, and favorite toys. She'd washed everything, but some items had seen better days. Still, they were familiar to him and might help him adjust easier.

The dog trotted next to her left side. The same as he usually did. He only pulled ahead of her occasionally. "You're doing so much better."

He rubbed against her, more like a cat than a large dog.

She scratched behind his ear. "I'm going to miss you."

Her throat burned, and her eyes stung.

Focus on what was best for Rascal.

She would cry later, when she added the final note to his page in her binder of the animals she'd fostered over the past six years. Some stayed at her house for a brief time, others for months, some until their time on earth ended. No matter if they were puppies or kitties, middle aged, or seniors, all were her "kiddos." She loved them—pouring her heart into each one no matter the length of time they'd lived with her. She wanted only what was best for her fosters, but here, now, she wished Rascal wasn't going to a new home. She wanted him to stay with her.

"I'm being selfish," she told him. "You'll be happy wherever you are and whomever you're with."

"I hope that's true."

The sound of Bryce's voice sent chills down her spine. She clutched the leash in her hand. "What are you doing here?"

"Picking up my new dog."

She gasped. "You're adopting Rascal?"

"You were right. The beast isn't so bad."

As if on cue, Rascal pulled her toward him. The dog didn't rear up, but he rubbed his muzzle against Bryce's leg.

"He seems to like you," she said.

"What about you?"

Bryce's words stopped her cold. She had no idea why he

was asking after what he'd accused her of. She raised her chin. "Does it matter after the way you spoke to me? The things you said?"

"I was a jerk."

"Yes, though I'm not sure I'd use a past tense verb if I were you."

"I deserve that. I sure don't deserve you." He took a step toward her, much to Rascal's delight and Dakota's dismay. "I was...am...an idiot. I hope you can forgive me for being, as my dad would call it, a total fool."

She hadn't expected this and wasn't sure what to say. "What made you act foolish?"

"Over a decade of guilt that only worsened when my mom died...and you."

Dakota drew back. "Me?"

"I came to this small town in Montana with one goal in mind. To take my father back to Seattle with me. Then I met you. You came bearing chocolate and dogs and had the most incredible smile I've ever seen."

Her heart rammed against her chest.

"You were funny and challenging. A pain and a pleasure. And somewhere between trying to find animals homes and sneaking kisses while the dogs weren't looking, I fell for you. Fell hard."

She sucked in a breath.

"All I've wanted since I arrived was to go home to Seattle. I thought I was doing us both a favor by acting like such an ass, but I realized after you told me goodbye, rightfully so, that I was home. This big-city boy is ready to give small-town living a try."

She opened her mouth to reply, but no words came out.

"I figured I needed a dog, and what better dog than one who needs as much work on manners as I do? Maybe we can learn from each other. Or find someone who can help us both. But I'm skipping the cowboy boots. Too uncomfortable. And not my style."

Her heart stumbled. His words brought a rush of emotions—from shock to anticipation to uncertainty to fear. "I don't know what to say."

"Good. I was worried you were going to tell me the boots are a deal breaker."

Now she was confused. "Deal?"

He held her free hand. "Do you know why Marietta is home?"

She swallowed around the lump in her throat. "Because your father lives here."

"Not just my dad." Bryce gazed into her eyes. "My family. My dad, Scout, Pierre, Rascal, and…you. If you'll have us. Me. I love you."

Dakota's knees went week. Until she remembered what he'd said to her. "The things you accused me of…it hurt…hurts."

"I know. And I am sorry. I was out of my head, acting crazy, not sure what to do or say. Like the times before, I let my emotions take over. Everything I said came out wrong. I knew what was happening at the time, but I believed walking away like that was better than a drawn-out goodbye would be when it was time for me to leave. If I could do it all over again differently, I would. I love you, Dakota. I really do. I'm ready to spend a lifetime showing you how much you mean to me."

Forget chocolate. Nothing could be as swoon-worthy as this.

But could she trust his words? Trust him?

"Still speechless?" he asked.

Dakota nodded. She wanted to jump into his arms but couldn't. "And afraid."

He raised her hand to his lips. "I don't ever want to hurt you again."

A shiver ran through her. She wanted to believe him. "The thing is I've fallen for false promises and careless declarations of love before. I'm not sure I'm ready to take another chance."

Playing it safe sounded really good to her and her heart. But the thought of losing Bryce threatened to rip her apart.

"I get it."

Did he? She wished he knew.

"Remember when I told you I never freak out?" he asked.

"You said except on extremely rare occasions."

"This was one of those occasions. A big one because of how much you mean to me." He caressed her face with the edge of his fingertip. "We haven't known each other long, and I hurt you. More than once. That was wrong of me. But I know this. I love you, Dakota Parker. I love how you do so much for everyone, friend or stranger, and for every animal who crosses your path. You put others first and that has ended up causing you pain. I can't promise that I won't screw up again. I probably will, but my feelings for you won't change. I want to put you first, to give you all the love you pour out to others, to help make your dreams come true. If you can see in your heart to forgive me yet again and let me have another chance."

Thinking about what might happen scared her. He'd hurt her, and her heart could easily be broken again, but the alternative—a life without Bryce—frightened her more. Because…she loved him.

Dakota took a breath. And another. "You can have another chance."

"Say that again."

"I'll give you another chance, but don't screw up." She said the words so loudly Rascal barked. That broke the tension, and she laughed. Time to take her own leap and risk it all. "Somewhere through all of this, I fell in love with you, too. I realized I've been using the animals to fill what was missing in my life. The chocolate, too. It doesn't have to be all or nothing. I can have balance in my life. I can take the time to fix up my house. I can…love."

They were both learning from each other.

He kissed her. A kiss full of longing and love. She couldn't get enough.

Dakota leaned against him. She soaked up the warmth and feel of him. He wasn't a perfect man, but he was special and the right man for her.

Rascal nudged between them.

Bryce laughed. "You're going to have to work with Rascal on this."

"Not me. Us."

"Us. I like the sound of that." With one hand on Rascal's head, Bryce kissed her again.

Epilogue

DINNER AT THE Graff Hotel was the best Thanksgiving dinner Bryce had eaten in years. Not only was his stomach full, but his heart was, too. He sat on his father's couch with Dakota next to him and Rascal at his feet. "The food at the Graff rivals the best meals I've had in Seattle."

Dakota shook her head. She looked at his dad. "Does he always compare everything to Seattle?"

"Yep." His father sat in his recliner with Pierre on his shoulder and Scout at his side. The three looked like a cozy trio. "We'll have to deprogram him when he returns with all his stuff. We're also going to have to get him to stop dressing like a city slicker who's only here for a visit."

Holding back laughter, Bryce feigned annoyance. "I can hear you."

"Good," his father replied. "Might motivate you to buy some new clothes."

"A pair of Wranglers, at least," Dakota joked.

Bryce gave her a look. "You said my clothes were nice."

"I gave in on you not wearing cowboy boots," she said.

"But jeans and a western shirt won't kill you."

He glanced at her outfit. "Interesting coming from a woman dressed more like a city girl in skinny jeans and ankle boots. Pretty hip for someone living in a small town."

"The boots belong to Portia."

Figures, but Dakota looked hot in them. Though he'd say the same thing if she were in a pair sweats, a hoodie, and flip-flops. "What about the skinny jeans?"

She raised her chin. "Those are mine, but women all over wear them."

"Not as well as you do, my dear," his father said.

"Thank you, Walt." Her mouth slanted into a wry grin. "I see how Bryce became such a charmer."

Walt nodded. "Takes after his old man."

These two, along with the three animals, were going to keep Bryce on his toes. He didn't mind one bit.

"I'm ready for a nap." His dad pulled the lever so he was more horizontal. "I'll just rest here with my new friends."

More like fur-covered kids, but Bryce wasn't going to say anything. He couldn't when Rascal followed him around the house like a shadow. Granted, the puppy hadn't been here long, but the dog had whined so much from his crate last night that Bryce let him sleep on his bed.

Not that Dakota would know that.

Still, Rascal seemed to enjoy sleeping with him, and the bedroom wasn't that worse for the wear in the morning. The dog was smart. In less than twenty-four hours, he'd learned to keep his distance from the man with the casts on his legs.

Instinct or Dakota's training?

Whichever, Bryce was not only pleased but also proud. He also knew the time had come to take the dog out. "Let's go for a walk with Rascal while my dad naps."

She stood. "Sounds great. I'd love to work off calories from dinner."

"Holiday calories don't count."

"Tell that to my waistline."

Bryce helped Dakota into her jacket, shrugged on his, and grabbed Rascal's leash.

The cool air refreshed him after eating so much food, but with each step he took, his nerves increased. He wanted to act cool and calm, as if this was any other Thursday in November, but he could barely breathe.

He knew something that might help. He laced his gloved hands with Dakota's.

The sun hung low in the sky, and the streetlamps hadn't turned on yet.

On Main Street, the only place opened was Grey's Saloon. Music played inside, and two cowboys walked into the bar.

He looked down the block. "Not much going on around here."

"That's Marietta for you."

"I'm getting used to the quiet. I like it," he said. "It's peaceful."

"Don't get too used it. The Marietta stroll will be coming up in a couple of weeks, and this street will be jam-packed with people."

"I'm looking forward to it."

They passed the Copper Mountain Gingerbread and Dessert Factory. A closed sign hung on the door. Thanksgiving desserts, including a pilgrim-inspired gingerbread montage, filled the window.

"I put a pumpkin pie in your fridge when I came over," Dakota said.

"Can't wait. Though my dad is probably hoping you brought more chocolate."

"I did."

"Always thinking of others."

"I planned on having both myself."

That made Bryce laugh. "So what happens now that the rescue is empty?"

"I'm guessing by tomorrow evening we'll have new residents."

"Bet you can't wait."

"Guilty as charged, but I won't go overboard with what I do there. I want to spend time with you and Rascal, work on the house, and make sure Walt is doing okay with Scout and Pierre."

Bryce liked the sound of that. "I want to keep volunteering at the rescue."

"Lori will be happy to hear that. I sure am."

The chocolate shop was up ahead. Other than marking every tree they passed, Rascal was relatively well behaved.

Still a beast, but Rascal was Bryce's beast, and he loved the pup.

Dakota stopped in front of the chocolate shop's window. She stared at the display. "Tomorrow, the turkeys, pilgrim hats, pumpkins, and maple leafs go into the sales basket. We won't see them for another year."

He placed his arm around her. "A year isn't that long."

Especially considering how fast November had been going by.

"I suppose not." She glanced at the dog. "Rascal will still be considered a puppy."

"I bet you'll be saying the same thing when he's twelve."

Dakota's brows drew together. Her lips parted, but she didn't say anything.

This seemed like the right time for what Bryce had been planning since yesterday.

"You love the chocolate shop and Rascal, so I thought here would be the perfect place to give you this." He reached into his pocket and pulled out a ring box. "I know you've had issues with men in the past, and I don't want you to have any doubts about my intentions. I'm here to stay. In Marietta. And with you.

"I love you, Dakota, and I want to be with you forever." He opened the box. A piece of paper was inside. "But after what I've put you through, I want you to take your time and not feel pushed into something. I designed a ring for you. When you're ready, I'll have it made. No rush."

She unfolded the piece of paper. Her eyes squinted, and then her mouth formed a perfect O. "That looks like a paw. It's perfect."

"Seemed fitting for us." He looked at Rascal, who was facing the opposite direction. Of course the dog was. Bryce laughed. "Maybe by the time you're ready for this next step, Rascal won't think I'm playing if I go down on one knee."

Her eyes gleamed. "Thank you."

"I also thought about what you said to me about giving thanks. I have something to add to my list of what I'm thankful for."

"What's that?"

"Your heart." He cupped her face with his hand. "That your heart can love a fool like me."

"Happy Thanksgiving, Bryce." She stared up at him with affection in her eyes. "Until you arrived in Marietta, I thought all I needed were chocolate and animals. I'm so thankful you showed me I needed more. You. I love you."

"I love you." And Bryce always would. He kissed her gently on the lips. A kiss to tell her what to look forward to—a life together, a family, and helping to make each other's dreams come true. "Happy Thanksgiving, Dakota."

The End

You'll love the next book in the…

Love at the Chocolate Shop series

Book 1: *Melt My Heart, Cowboy* by C.J. Carmichael
Book 2: *A Thankful Heart* by Melissa McClone
Book 3: *Montana Secret Santa* by Debra Salonen
Book 4: *The Chocolate Cure* by Roxanne Snopek
Book 5: *The Valentine Quest* by Melissa McClone
Coming soon

The rest of the Love at the Chocolate Shop is coming soon!

More by *USA Today* Bestselling author Melissa McClone

The Bar V5 Ranch series

Fall in love at the Bar V5 Dude Ranch in Montana

Book 1: *Home For Christmas*
Book 2: *Mistletoe Magic*
Book 3: *Kiss Me, Cowboy*
Book 4: *Mistletoe Wedding*
Book 5: *A Christmas Homecoming*

Available now at your favorite online retailer!

About the Author

USA Today Bestselling author **Melissa McClone** has published over twenty-five novels with Harlequin and been nominated for Romance Writers of America's RITA award. She lives in the Pacific Northwest with her husband, three school-aged children, two spoiled Norwegian Elkhounds and cats who think they rule the house. For more on Melissa's books, visit her website: www.melissamcclone.com

Thank you for reading

A Thankful Heart

If you enjoyed this book, you can find more from all our great authors at TulePublishing.com, or from your favorite online retailer.

Made in the USA
Las Vegas, NV
14 July 2022

51626205R00155